Attack of the Giant Bugs

A.J. & Eli Ponder

Attack of the Giant Bugs

A.J & Eli Ponder

Attack Of The Giant Bugs

with over 25 endings to amaze, delight and horrify

Someone needs to stop Jeremy Wilder the Bugman from taking over the city of Greenville, and indeed the whole world – it should be YOU!

YOU are Greenville's only hope. You choose which path you take. You can fail your mission or succeed your wildest expectations. But beware, within these pages lies great danger – giant bugs, ants, ladybirds, praying mantises and more. You might come to a grizzly end, or be transformed but whatever happens a real hero keeps fighting, even after they fail.

Are you ready?

Yes! I want to go straight to the story, so I can save Greenville and be the hero I was meant to be.

Go to page 6

Dedicated to YOU

Let your bravery save the world!

Introduction: School Trip

New teacher. New school. The weirdest school you've ever been to. Ms Xavier, next door, runs her class like a military academy, while your teacher, Mr Adams is soft as cheese. The bell rang five minutes ago, and half the class aren't even sitting down.

Mr Adams strums his guitar. "Gather round. We're going to go on a primo museum trip with class Xavier." He gets up, still strumming his guitar. "Hey, let's have a singalong as we walk to the bus stop."

No one actually sings as the class straggles to the bus stop, accompanied by Mr Adams plunking. Some students are arguing about who's going to get into the most trouble – Frankie or Steve. Whoever they are.

Ms Xavier, the other class teacher, is standing next to the bus stop already. She's wearing a stiff brown suit buttoned up to her neck, and shoes so sensible they could be army issue. Maybe she is ex-army – her hawkish gaze is enough to keep her class in military rows.

Your new friend Kennedy nudges you, and points to a girl at the back of Ms Xavier's queue. "Hey, that's the

Frankie. Watch out, her inventions are dangerous. Last year, her Homeworkulator Delux ate my homework and exploded." Since you arrived at Greenville High, you've heard stories about Frankie, the mad inventor. And Kennedy's not the only one. Someone is always talking about Frankie's exploits. Crazy stories about her shrinking the class to the size of insects, and making some kind of hot air balloon that swallowed half Mrs McGinty's class and terrified the school. Of course, you don't believe a word. Surely it would have made the news or something?

Besides, Frankie doesn't look anything special – short hair, flannel shirt, and jean pockets with bits of wire sticking out.

A tall boy, his face covered in spots, scurries up. The backpack slung low over his shoulder hits his butt as he walks.

"Steve. Detention!" Ms Xavier snaps.

He shrugs nonchalantly, like he gets detention every day. Somehow, he's also immune to Ms Xavier's queue.

Nobody seems to notice, except Kennedy, who rushes over and winks, "Hey, bad luck. Detention again." She grins. "Can I have detention too, Ms Xavier?"

Weird, who'd want detention?

Besides, if Kennedy's ditching you, maybe it's time to find out more about this Frankie. "Hi," you say as the bus pulls up. It has an overpowering bus-smell of farts and grease.

Frankie keeps tinkering with her phone – no, whatever it is, it's longer and narrower than a phone – more like a remote control. She doesn't seem that friendly, but when you clamber onto the bus, there aren't exactly heaps of seats left. So you hunker in beside her near the back. Mr Adams is crammed onto the back seat with half a dozen students. They're singing some awful school song.

Ms Xavier moves into the seat across from you and Frankie. She keeps on looking over, as if you're about to catch on fire. Or as if Frankie is.

Whenever Ms Xavier isn't looking, Frankie's tinkering with the strange remote.

"Hi," you say again, kind of awkwardly. Being the new kid sucks.

"Hi," she says. "I'm Frankie. Don't mind me. I'm just working on an old invention. It's almost there." She pulls out a mini-screwdriver. "Just have to tighten the last few screws."

"So what is it?" you whisper, glancing across to Ms Xavier. She's busy telling someone off. Probably for breathing wrong.

"It was a shrink ray," Frankie says. "But now it's a transmogrification ray. If you press this button, it should re-size almost anything it's pointed at. But don't press the black button, that's transmogrification. It could change you into a mouse, and once that happens, you might not turn human again."

"Well, don't point it at me."

She laughs. "No, I thought I'd try it out at the museum. On something small. Like an ant. Or a cockroach"

The bus drives up to the museum entrance, and Ms Xavier rushes to the front of the bus. "Step to it," she says. "No dawdling. Last person out empties the trash for the whole semester."

Kennedy throws her a salute as she bustles past.

"Behave yourself, Kennedy, or you'll be begging to empty those bins," Ms Xavier snaps.

Kennedy grins back, and salutes. "Yes, Ms Xavier, sir!"

Jeremy Wilder at the Museum

You and Kennedy are the last to walk through the revolving doors of the Greenville Natural History Museum and into the foyer. A weirdly-thin guy in a museum t-shirt is introducing himself to the class. "Hi, I'm Jeremy Wilder. People call me, the Bugman," he says with crazed glee. "I'm your guide for today. So, come with me and we'll explore the creepy-crawly world of bugs."

You're walking along with Frankie, when Jeremy Wilder reaches out and snatches Frankie's transmogrification remote. "No cell phones or devices," he says. "It's on your permission form."

"Give it back, now," Frankie demands.

"Hey," Kennedy says. "You can't take cell phones off us."

"Or our transmogrifiers!" Frankie yells. "They're dangerous."

"Hey—" you yell, but Jeremy Wilder's already walking away, holding the device high above his head. "I'm sorry, I'll just be a moment. I have to check this with, um, security."

"That's bull," Frankie yells loud enough that Mr Adams and Ms Xavier can hear through a class of noisy students. Ms Xavier barely turns around from reading an information plaque. "Whatever it is, it can wait," she says adjusting her reading glasses with a worried frown.

Mr Adams doesn't even turn around. No surprise there.

"The display is straight ahead," Jeremy Wilder says. "Go on through." He points to a huge room packed with bug displays, cabinets and terrariums, then disappears behind a door with a large sign that says, Museum Staff Only, taking the transmogrifier.

"I'm going to get my transmogrifier back," Frankie says. "You coming?" She looks over at Ms Xavier who's talking to Steve in angry whispers.

"Coast's clear," Frankie says, and pushes her way through the door.

Do you:

Follow Frankie through the blue staff only door? P14

Or

Stay with the class? P12

Stay With the Class

You walk past a colourful display of Bugs of the Antipodes. There are pictures and small models of spiders and insects, including a life-sized weta. But the human-sized models of common garden insects in the centre of the room really stand out. Closest is a giant fly. Its fluorescent blue and green body glows beautifully, but the model's underbelly is dark and spiky and its brownish-red eyes appear to follow you around the room. Creepy. There's also an enormous ladybird, a spiky stick insect and a very fluffy bumblebee.

Below each model is a digital plaque covered with information. Kennedy is hunched over one, busy working. No. Kennedy never works. Everybody knows that. Even you, and you're the new kid. You look a little closer. She's waving a purple fluorescent light at the screen and making notes.

23-15-19 13-5-5-20-9-14-7 20-8-18-15-21-7-8
7-18-5-5-14 5-13-5-18-7-5-14-3-25 4-15-15-18

Kennedy's not writing about the bugs, but writing down the numbers. Weird. She's being careful to cover the words under the numbers – but you catch the last word in the sentence as she writes each letter – D-O-O-R.

Okay, that's weird.

There's a flash as the lights flare and die. The room is lit in the green glow of emergency exit signs. "Hey, what's up with the lights?" Mr Adams asks, stumbling around in the semi-darkness.

Kennedy and a couple of her friends have disappeared. There must be at least five people missing, including Frankie.

Ms Xavier shrugs as the lights flicker back to life. "Let's get on with the bug tour," she snaps. "No need to make a fuss. You should be taking plenty of notes for your projects." Hasn't she noticed that some of the students have disappeared?

Ms Xavier pulls out her phone. While she's distracted, you could sneak away to see what Kennedy and the others are up to.

You look around. There are three ways you could go – sneak out a blue door, sneak out a green door, or continue through the archway to the next part of the exhibit. If you go through one of the doors, you might find Frankie, or Kennedy and the others, but if you continue on, there's a good chance you'll see more amazing bugs.

You have three choices. ***Do you***:

Sneak through the blue door. **P14**
Or
Sneak through the green door. **P34**
Or
Continue through to see the rest of the exhibit. **P124**

Sneak Through the Blue Door

On the other side of the blue door is a short corridor. Signs above point to the foyer and bathrooms You spend a few minutes exploring, but there's nothing to do. So you wander back to the doorway. Before you even open it, you hear Ms Xavier shouting from the other side. "No! You can't do this to my students."

Carefully, you open the door a crack and peek through. She's yelling at a weirdly-thin dude in an ugly grasshopper face-mask. Behind him, a giant white bowling pin wobbles.

A bowling pin?

Good on Ms Xavier, she might be full of vinegar, but she's standing in front of the Bugman, protecting everyone, while Mr Adams is…where is Mr Adams? Oh, he's cowering behind an exhibit, clutching his guitar.

Students shriek in fear. What's happening? You open the door a little wider. For a split second Ms Xavier is standing inside a beam of light coming from a remote that's being waved about by the skinny guy in the ugly grasshopper face-mask. Then she disappears.

"Ms Xavier's gone!" Someone yells. "Kidnapped! Murdered! Blasted to a million pieces! What are we going to do?"

You hold your hand over your mouth to stop from gasping.

"No one dare defy me, I am the Bugman. Together, my bugs and I are going to take over the world!"

Where is Frankie?

Thinking about Frankie reminds you of her remote. Maybe Ms Xavier isn't really dead, or blasted to a million pieces. If the Bugman's remote is Frankie's transmogrifier, she could just be very small. Then you realise the giant white bowling pin behind the Bugman is Frankie. You can just see her face sticking out of swaths of the sticky white stuff coating her body. Spider web?

The Bugman orders everyone to pick up a terrarium and carry it out through the emergency exit. Because you've been so quiet, he doesn't notice you peeking through the doorway.

Soon they're all gone. Even Frankie.

Do you:

Rush through the emergency exit to rescue the class? P16

Or

Try and find Ms Xavier? If she's been shrunk maybe you can sneak after the class together? **P18**

Rush Through the Emergency Exit to Rescue the Class

In your hurry, you crash into Frankie. She's being carried by three people.

The weirdly-skinny Bugman stops mid-rant and turns to face you "Mwah ha ha ha. You cannot stop the Bugman." He points the remote at you and the world spirals sickeningly, like you've been spun around in a dryer. Everything grows and grows until even the grass is taller than you are.

Something's moving through the giant blades of grass. A shiny reddish-brownish creature.

A centipede. Its spiky jaws open as it scuttles toward you.

You run, fighting against the thick grass.

Behind you, the creature, its many legs moving in waves, scurries faster than you ever could.

Your heart beats in terror. You duck behind a twig, gasping for breath.

The twig's twice as big as you.

The centipede pulls away, shiny segments closing up like a squeezed accordion.

You breathe a sigh of relief. Surely you're safe now.

The creature launches itself so fast it's like a thunderbolt descending. It grabs you in its jaws and raises you off the ground, flooding your body with poison. Your vision grows black. All your senses numb.

I'm sorry, you've been eaten. The world of bugs is a dangerous one, with plenty of wonderful opportunities to die horribly. When you head out on a new adventure you may like to die a hideous death again, become a spy and learn how to crack codes, raise dragons in the country, or help invent a machine that twists time and allows you to have many, many adventures.

Now your adventure is over, you have three choices:

Go back to *Jeremy Wilder at the Museum*. P10

Or

Discover what would have happened if you'd tried to find Ms Xavier first. P18

Or

Go to the Adventure Contents and choose any part of the adventure. P184

Try and Find Ms Xavier

Maybe you can Sneak after the Class Together

While you're searching the floor for Ms Xavier, you wonder about Frankie's transmogrifier. How can such a machine work? But why else would Jeremy Wilder take it? And who else could the Bugman be? It's a shame you didn't get a closer look.

Shrink rays, really? Just as you're thinking maybe the whole class is making a fool of you, you see something. A tiny green and brown figure. It's wearing the same earthy colours as Ms Xavier. And it's totally the wrong shape for an insect.

You kneel down. Yes, it's definitely her.

Cautiously, you put your hand out and she climbs on.

She's talking in a high-pitched whisper that's hard to understand.

You put her up to your ear. "What are you waiting for?" she squeaks, the sound worse than feedback. "We need to rescue the class!"

"Good idea."

She claps her hands over her ears.

"Right, sorry," you whisper, "I'll try not to talk so loud."

Putting Ms Xavier in your pocket, you race out the emergency exit. You're just in time to see the rest of your class disappearing into a tunnel in front of an elephant statue. The tunnel door is closing as you exit the museum.

As you run across the lawn the hatch clicks shut. You pull. It was open just moments ago, but the tunnel door will not open.

"I know how to get into this," Ms Xavier's tiny voice says. "All you have to do is press the toenails in the right order."

Toenails? Oh, the elephant's toenails. Suspicious, you place her near the foot of the elephant. She points out the second toe, and then the third. You press them because she's not strong enough. "Now one and four, and four again."

When you press the last toe, the hatch opens so smoothly you can barely hear the hum of an electric motor. You grab Ms Xavier and put her safely back in your pocket, then take the steps down into the long corridor.

The door closes behind you, leaving you in the dark. But not as dark as you first thought. There's light sneaking from under some of the doors lining the dim corridor – just enough to see the walls are covered with posters.

Muffled voices are nearby. Are they friends, or enemies? Most likely enemies. This is a secret bunker hideout.

You sneak down the stairs, and into the corridor, glancing into the various rooms, trying to find your classmates.

Footsteps echo behind you.

You run, almost colliding with a figure standing in the shadows.

An arm reaches out and grabs you.

You look to see who it is… “Kennedy?”

“Shh, you’ll blow our cover,” she whispers.

“Someone’s behind me!” you pant.

“Don’t worry, that’s only Greg. He’s been working undercover as a janitor here for months.

“Hey Greg,” says Kennedy. “It looks like Ms Xavi— I mean, the Chief’s not coming. It’s a shame, but we’re going to have to go in without her.”

“What?” Greg says. “We can’t go in without the Chief. This is her World of Spies operation. And it’s much bigger than we thought.”

“World of Spies?” you say. It’s kind of weird in here. Recruitment signs for WOE are everywhere, but World of Spies would be WOS.

“Oh dear,” Ms Xavier says. “The World of Evil has been busy.”

Nobody else seems to hear.

It’s difficult to know what to do. Should you trust these crazy people? Are they really part of the World of Spies? You can’t be sure, but either way, you have a choice.

Do you:

Say you have Ms Xavier in your pocket? P21
Or
Keep quiet and don’t mention Ms Xavier. P26

Say you Have Ms Xavier in Your Pocket

"I know where Ms Xavier is," you say, pulling her out of your pocket.

"So she's shrunk," Greg mutters, eyeing the tiny Ms Xavier cupped in your hands. "Frankie needs to keep a better eye on her inventions."

"Shh, Greg," Kennedy hisses. "You'll blow our cover."

"Hey," Ms Xavier calls. "We need to go left, then right, then left again. And we need to move quickly. The good news is, we know what WOE is up to. The bad news is, the Bugman's helped them, and they're massively ahead of schedule. Now, put me on your shoulder, I'm not going back in that pocket."

You put her on your shoulder, and continue following her directions until an ant the size of a German Shepherd comes galloping toward you, jaws snapping. It's horrifying.

"Quick, in there," Ms Xavier calls. She points to a door.

Kennedy woggles a stick with spikes around in the lock. "I can't get it open."

"Focus," Ms Xavier snaps.

At last, the door clicks open.

"There we are," Kennedy says, rushing you through the door. "Sorry, nerves must have got the better of me."

Inside the room are a line of cells. Inside the cells are Frankie, most of the students from the school trip, and some museum staff. You can tell they're museum staff because of their brightly coloured bug t-shirts with the museum logo.

Kennedy rushes to unlock Frankie's cell, and then makes her way around all the cells to free everyone – including Mr Adams, who is cradling a broken guitar. As you go to help, the newly-rescued Frankie pulls you aside.

"Do you know where Ms Xavier is? I have some very important information for her."

"Of course," you say.

Ms Xavier squeaks, "I'm right here."

"Oh, sorry," Frankie mumbles. She stares at your shoulder. "Is that really you, Ms Xavier?"

Ms Xavier waves her arMs "Who do you think it is?"

"Good. I've designed a cancellation device, but I need some help from WOS. Can they broadcast this infrasonic signal? We need to get it transmitted over the whole museum."

She presses the play button on her phone. You don't hear anything, but Ms Xavier starts to grow.

You fall over, half crushed by Ms Xavier before she rolls away like an action star.

"Frankie! You could have given us some warning!" she yells.

"But I did warn you." Frankie says. She explains using technobabble so dense even Einstein would have trouble understanding.

"Never mind that." Ms Xavier brushes herself off. "Let me just turn on my encrypted connection and we'll have your anti-transmogrifying signal broadcasting in no time."

"Awesome," Kennedy says. "For a while there, I thought we weren't going to survive this. But it's going to be easy now." She grins around at everyone. "And it's all thanks to my new bestie."

Does she mean best friend? Probably. You hope so. Some of the class are tittering. Is that good or bad?

"Well done," Ms Xavier says. "Come on though, we still have to save the day!" Everyone traipses down the WOS corridor into a room full of screens and together you put the Bugman under arrest. It's easy now that he doesn't have any giant ants. Besides, Ms Xavier even has handcuffs. She lets you put them on the Bugman, before the police turn up.

A policewoman gives Kennedy the stink eye. "I hope you're not getting into trouble, Kennedy Stevenson?" she says.

"I've been perfect, Mum, why don't you ask Ms Xavier?"

"A delight," Ms Xavier says, ignoring the officer's

glare. "I don't suppose you'll mind, but this has been very stressful on all the students." She looks around. Half of them do look upset. They're the half from your class. Mr Adams says, "Come on class. We'll get back to school. I know this has been stressful, but we'll all feel better when I get my second guitar and we'll have a chat and a sing along."

Ms Xavier has a quick word with him. Apparently she wants you and Kennedy to be in her class. "Come on, this is going to be fun," she says. "We're going to have a party."

She buys everyone a pizza, and then half the class goes home, but she says she wants a word with the rest of you. There's lots of nudging and winking going on. What is this? It's not a prank is it?

No! It's a celebration. You're brought to the World of Spies headquarters, where they shower you with praise for saving Ms Xavier, or Chief X, as she likes to be called. Then someone in a dark suit gives you a certificate that looks like a piece of paper - until you wave a black light over it underneath a full moon. There's a big long boring speech, of course, but nobody else is listening either. It's pretty obvious you're not the only person playing with a World of Spies' gizmo when a flash of light scorches the podium. You look around and see a boy playing with a laser lipstick.

"Right," Ms Xavier says. "I can see we still have discipline probleMs Detention for a month."

The whole room erupts in cheers and wolf-whistles.

You look confused and Kenney whispers to you, “That means more training.”

Now you’ve been made an honorary member of the World of Spies, you have access to the most amazing gadgets you could ever imagine, and plenty of opportunities to save the world. Still, with adventure only a heartbeat away, sometimes you wonder what other choices you might have made on the fateful day of your museum trip.

Serving your ant masters, throwing exploding gum at ladybirds, even becoming an author of tall tales – or, to be more precise, terrifying tales about very small creatures.

For more adventure, click on a link to:

Go back to *Jeremy Wilder at the Museum*. P10

Or

Go to the Adventure Contents and choose any path. P184

Keep Quiet and Don't Mention Ms Xavier

The more you think about it, the happier you are with your decision not to mention Ms Xavier. For a start, you don't know this janitor guy. What if he's working with the Bugman? And why is Kennedy here, anyway?

You might not trust these two, but you do want to find the rest of your class, so you stick with them.

Because she's so small, they don't notice Ms Xavier jump out of your pocket. You bend down to hear what's she's yelling, but it's hard to understand with her voice all squeaky from being so small. Maybe she's talking about the posters for WOE. Or maybe it's something else. Before you can figure it out, you hear.

And then you see it. A huge ant, as black and shiny as Darth Vader's dog, scurries through a door at the end of the corridor. It's the size of a German Shepherd, and it's coming your way, fast.

Kennedy is scrabbling in her pockets. She turns to the janitor. "I don't suppose you could help?"

The fake janitor guy points something at the creature. Lipstick? It flashes, singeing the ant.

The corridor stinks of burnt hair.

"Holey socks!" the janitor yells and starts fiddling with the dial.

Time freezes. Or it just seems to go really slowly as the giant ant continues toward you, jaws opening. You hit the armored creature as hard as you can. "Ow!" The armor plating on that thing is tough! You hit it again.

It doesn't seem to notice your blows and scoops you up with its spiky jaws.

You scream and flail, desperate for it to let you go, but it's gripping you so tight, it's drawing blood. Ow! Ow! Ow!

With you firmly in its jaws, it runs back down the corridor. One moment you can see every little detail, even read the posters. The next, you're flashing past a doorway.

More ants arrive. Lots more ants. They swarm Kennedy and Greg, the fake janitor. Kennedy throws something and an ant blows up. But that doesn't stop the ants for long, it just makes them angry.

Soon there are bits of Kennedy and Greg the fake janitor all over the corridor.

You kick and punch harder than ever, not that the ant notices.

You scream.

Still nothing. The ant only stops when it reaches a big room filled with screens.

You're dropped at the Bugman's feet.

"Ah." He grins. "Nice of you to drop by." Then he laughs at his own terrible joke, leans over you, and yells, "Join me or die."

Do you:

Say you'll join the Bugman? P29

Or

Tell the Bugman you'd rather die? *Warning, this ending is too scary for one of the authors!* P31

Say You'll Join the Bugman

You smile up at the Bugman as non-threateningly as you can. "Of course, I'll join you. Where do I sign up?"

The Bugman walks to a set of honeycomb shaped drawers and pulls out a wad of paper, then roars with laughter. "You think minions get health insurance? You do the job or you die." He gives you a dustpan and brush. "Now here's the giant ant pooper scooper. Your job is to keep this bunker clean."

Two ants chaperone you around the building. At first it's not so bad, but more dangerous giant insects are arriving, every day, every hour, and every minute. The drudgery and the smell are overwhelmingly terrible. Not only is there more and more bug poop, but the more insects there are around the Bugman, the less chance someone will get close enough to overthrow him.

As you rush off to clean more ant poop, you can't help thinking how unfair life is now that the Bugman has taken over the world and declared himself Grand Ruler and the Greatest Entomologist in the World. To make it worse, Ms Xavier has disappeared without a word. You're not sure when. It was probably on the first day when you agreed to become a World of Evil minion. There are rumors that she hates WOS more than anything, and that she's out riding ants somewhere and enjoying her life as a miniature spy.

Your fellow minions also whisper the codename for a courageous inventor working hard to invent a machine to return Mr Wilder's bugs to their proper size. Frankenstein. Others say the inventor is Frankie, and she's going to release her device any day now. There are more whispers that she's dead. It's hard to have any hope in this terrible bug-infested new world. It's all whispers and innuendo. Almost nobody dares step out of line, and the ones that do are eaten by the Bugman's ant militia.

Now you have little to do but pick up ant poop, you have plenty of time to reflect. Maybe it could have gone differently, if only more people had resisted earlier. If only you had. With a different choice you could have become a world-class spy, a famous entomologist, or even had the honor of dying one of many horrible deaths that lurk in the Bugman's world. Sometimes, during a mission, an attack of either acute stupidity or rampant bravery is required. Which is why, win or lose, you should celebrate taking a stand. Besides, in an adventure like this, isn't gore half the fun?

To help you on your way would you like to:

Start again at *Jeremy Wilder at the Museum*? P10
Or
Find out what happens if you stand up to the Bugman and say you'd rather die? (*Scary ending!*) **P31**

Tell the Bugman You'd Rather Die –

WARNING, THIS ENDING IS TOO SCARY FOR ONE OF THE AUTHORS!

"I'd rather die than join you," you yell.

"Good on you," Ms Xavier squeaks. (She's climbed in your ear and it's tickling.)

"Awesome." The Bugman grins. "I was hoping you'd say that. We'll feed you to the giant and lins."

"The giant and what?"

"Giant antlions. Don't you know what antlions are? Where do you kids get your education from? Cornflakes packets? Or plain old-fashioned state-sanctioned indoctrination?"

Struggling and protesting, you're dragged into a mini-stadium with a huge sandpit in the middle. Once, it must have been a pool with blue tiles edging the water. Now, there's nothing but sand sloping down into a large pit in the centre.

You're led right up to the tile edging.

Sand moves at the bottom of the pit. No, it's not just sand, there's something down there.

You stare at the giant funnel of sand in horror. "No!" you yell, struggling to get away.

"Mwah ha ha ha, not likely." The Bugman pushes you into the pit.

You fall and land sprawling, Ms Xavier holding tight to your ear. As you try to get up, the sand slides out from under you and you fall again, tumbling down the slope toward the dark nightmare shadow and black spindly limbs below.

"Slow, but sure," Ms Xavier squeaks.

You right yourself, and begin to crawl.

Sand cascades beneath you, but you're making progress – slow but sure. Ignoring the friction burns on your hands and knees you doggedly keep going, climbing just a little faster than the sand is sliding away.

A glob of sand hits you.

Ouch! You look back.

The horrible, spindly-legged antlion stares at you, snapping its mandibles.

You scurry harder.

Another glob of sand. It lands in front of you, starting a mini avalanche. Sand's collapsing around you, under you. No matter how hard you scrabble, the sand slides down carrying you right into the long chitinous limbs of the hungry antlion.

Up close, it's even uglier. Those limbs are very strong, and hard.

You fight valiantly, hitting and kicking it as hard as you can.

Ms Xavier's fighting too. She tries to defend you with her miniature handbag, but the antlion doesn't even see her as she bashes at its eyes.

The antlion's jaws pierce your chest.

You scream. Then you scream even louder as you realise the hollow jaws are acting like straws – and the coldblooded antlion is drinking you alive like a giant smoothie.

The last thing you hear is Ms Xavier saying your brave and your noble death will not be in vain.

(This does, in fact, turn out to be true. While you were distracting the Bugman with your untimely death, Ms Xavier's young spies were able to infiltrate the Bugman's lair and destroy much of his equipment. When Ms Xavier does eventually escape, she manages to organise her spies and all the good people of Greenville using a bodged ham radio. Together, they save Greenville from the Bugman's giant insects. But Ms Xavier never forgets your bravery, or that your actions were the turning point that stopped the Bugman from taking over the whole world. So she commissions a statue of you to be placed in the town square with the words, "Never Surrender" engraved underneath.

I'm sorry, you've been eaten by an antlion. The world of bugs is a dangerous one, which is what makes it so exciting. Next time, when you head out on adventure, you may like to die a hideous death or join the bad guys – on the other hand it might be fun to save the world like you did here. And even better if you can live to tell the tale.

For more adventure, click on a link to:

Go back to *Jeremy Wilder at the Museum*? P10
Or
Go to the Adventure Contents and choose any path. P184

Sneak Through the Green Door

On the other side, Kennedy and Greg and two students you don't really know are talking in terse whispers.

"Hi." You wave to Kennedy.

"Where do you think you're going?" Greg mutters, as if he's the boss of everyone.

"Quiet, Greg," Kennedy says. "Hey, awesome, you figured out the code."

(If you didn't figure out the code, you can go back and solve it now or leave it for another time. No one will know. If you want help, or enjoy codes, keep an eye out for the You join WOS as a spy ending, for code-cracking ideas.)

"You must be coming for the meeting," Kennedy says.

What meeting?

Nobody notices your confusion. They shine their torches on the walls to reveal ultraviolet arrows that glow under the torchlight and stride off along the corridor. You follow, until they come to a top outside an office door marked in ultraviolet, fluorescent pen: *Top Secret. World of Shoes business only (phones optional).* Raised voices are coming from inside. You can't quite hear what they're saying, but

it doesn't sound like it's about shoes. Not unless they're arguing about shoes that've disappeared, or been stolen or something.

Kennedy hesitates, but you're curious, so you push the door open. Ten people are arguing in strained voices, like they're trying and failing to keep quiet. You recognise Steve. How did he get here so fast?

He turns to look at you, and then resumes arguing. "Let's wait just a little longer for Chief X, then we..."

Chief X? Could that be Ms Xavier? The uptight school-teacher? Or maybe it's a relation of hers? It's hard to think of Ms Sensible Shoes Xavier as a spy. Still, not many people's names start with X.

Steve stands up and wipes the back of his hand over his pimply forehead. "This was supposed to be a practice." His voice cracks. "But now we have an emergency. I've just received an SOS alert from Chief X. Only, it was cut off midstream, and now I can't reach her at all."

Everyone starts talking at once.

"Let's rescue the Chief."

"We need to cordon off the building."

"No, we have a mission."

"What about Frankie's transmogrifier?" you ask. "The one the Bugman stole."

"What? Frankie's silly trans-mouse-ifier?" Steve says. "Why are you worried about that? Oh heck, it's a shrink ray too, isn't it? That means it could shrink Ms X. Or turn her into a mouse. Or anything!"

"No, just a mouse," Kennedy says. "Well, that and the shrink ray bit."

You nod in agreement. That's what Frankie said on the bus.

"Well, we can't just stand here," Greg says. "We have to do something, and quick!"

"You've convinced me," Steve says. "Let's get Frankie's device back from the Bugman, that thing's dangerous."

"No. We need to know what's happened to Chief X." Kennedy looks around.

They all start arguing again.

"Yeah, the Chief could still be alive."

"We shouldn't be looking for her. Not while the Bugman is loose."

"We need the Chief back, now!"

"No," Greg says. "We need to do her proud. So we're going to cordon off the building—

"And send a team in after the Bugman," Steve insists.

"No," Kennedy says. "I'm going to find Frankie and Ms Xavier. Oops. I mean Chief X." She turns bright red.

So Chief X is Ms Xavier. It might be a good idea to stay on her good side.

"Alright," Greg says. "I think you're both right. So can we have volunteers for both missions? And I'll organise

with WOS and get this place cordoned off. Everyone else, you need to decide if you'll help Kennedy find the Chief, or join Steve to find the Bugman?

Do you:

Volunteer to help Steve find the Bugman. P38

Or

Volunteer to help Kennedy find Ms Xavier and Frankie. P55

Volunteer to Help Steve Find the Bugman

"Thank you, everyone," Steve says. "You should all know me, I'm Steve. But some of us are new, so—" He nods at you and looks pointedly across at a boy with patched jeans, scraggly red hair, and a shirt that's way too big for him.

"Hi, I'm Murray," the boy says. "Homeschooled."

"Megan," says a girl with curly brown hair. She turns to you. "Stick with me, I'll keep you safe." She pulls a lipstick from a mini purse. "Here, I'll show you low beam." She points it to the wall. A red dot appears – it doesn't look like much, but it blackens and burns right through. "Whoops, I must have forgotten to calibrate it," she says. "Still, it'll be good in a pinch. Who'd like a Taser ring?"

She hands a gold ring to Murray, who is suitably impressed.

"A laser pen? Anybody?"

"Don't worry about me – I've got plenty," Steve says.

Megan turns back and hands the pen to you. "Be careful not to touch that button, unless it's an emergency," she says. "That's the overkill setting. And point it away from us. WOS insists on responsible laser usage."

"Oh, and here they are: my explosive packets of chewing gum. I've enough for one each. Also useable as cell phones – our emergency number's already preloaded – 0118 999 881 999 119 725 3."

You grasp the pen and a packet of chewing gum – carefully.

Steve puts on a pair of ultra-dark glasses and ushers you all down the corridor. How he can see through them is a complete mystery – until you notice they're working as TV screens and one of the screens shows him an enhanced view of the corridor. The others flick back and forth to show various rooMs Some you recognise from school, others are from the museum, and some you've never seen before.

"Incoming bug!" Steve yells.

"A ladybug! It's so cute," Megan says.

"You mean, Ladybird!" Murray squeals. "Run for your lives! Ladybirds can devour fifty aphids a day – and we're the size of aphids."

The ladybug darts after him, its wings whirring as loud as a helicopter.

Steve ducks, but he can't get out of the way. The ladybug is going to drop right on top of him.

Megan runs to his rescue, putting her schoolbag between the ladybug and Steve.

Bashing Megan's bag aside, the ladybug sinks its jaws into Steve's arm.

Blood pours from the wound and drips to the floor.

You have a choice:

Throw the exploding chewing gum at the ladybug. P41
Or
Race up to fight off the Ladybug with your laser pen. P59

Throw the Exploding Chewing Gum at the Ladybird

It's a good throw. The chewing gum hits the wing shell of the ladybug. "Hooray," you shout, moments before the chewing gum bounces off the wing shell and explodes on the corridor wall.

You dive away, protecting your head from the debris falling all around.

The roar of the explosion dies away and is replaced by the sound of a helicopter. No, not a helicopter. It's the ladybug rapidly beating its wings. They blur, and the enormous creature flies off.

Steve sits up, coughing. He's covered in soot and plaster, blood is dripping down his arm, and his hair is standing up on end. "Watch what you're doing, next time," he says. And winks. "Wouldn't like to die or anything. At least not so soon after being heroically rescued from a giant ladybug."

"Hey, look," Megan says, pointing to a huge smoking hole in the wall. Frankie and three scientists are on the other side. They've been tied to chairs with masses of shiny white stuff, but despite everything, they're still arguing.

"It can be done. I did it in first grade," Frankie muttered. "It has to be done, so we can shrink the insects back."

"Of course it can't be done," a bearded man with glasses snaps back. Then he looks up, his glasses slipping down his nose. "Finally, someone to rescue us. Thank goodness, we won't be eaten by lionants, I mean antlions."

"No need to worry about that," Steve says, kicking and punching at the the hole in the wall until it's just big enough for him to push through to the other side. Still covered in soot and plaster, he poses heroically, while you, Murray and Megan hurry through the Steve-shaped hole to free Frankie and the scientists.

"Ew," Megan says. "This stuff is really sticky."

"And stretchy," you say. It's almost impossible to pull away from the scientists, without it snapping right back. Globs of gluey stuff sticking to your hands make the job even more difficult.

"Spider web," Frankie says. "Burning would work best."

"Not with us in it," a bearded guy snaps. "What are you thinking?"

Carefully, you and Megan start using the laser to cut strands as you pull them away. They're almost free, when one of the scientists screams and points.

Ants are swarming into the room,

The Bugman is close on their heels. "Mwah ha ha ha," he says. "Let me make it simple for you, you can join me or die. Go line up next to the far wall with your hands up, and I won't set my giant ants on you."

You look left and right. Two of the scientists nervously shuffle toward the wall. Steve puts his hand in his pocket and steps toward the Bugman. "Would like some chewing gum?"

It's time to make a decision. Do you:

Put your hands up and stand by the wall with the two scientists? P44

Or

Stay with Steve and defy Bugman? P52

Put Your Hands Up and Stand By the Wall with the Two Scientists

You're shuffling to the wall when Steve repeats his offer. "Gum?" He offers the Bugman a whole packet of WOS brand gum.

An ant intercepts, its jaws closing on the strip as Steve lets go and jumps away.

The gum explodes in a wave of sound and debris.

Your ears are ringing. There are bits of ant everywhere. The walls and floor, everything. Steve and Murray are wiping their faces.

The remaining ants go crazy, tearing people apart. Steve is the first to go. With your ears still buzzing from the blast, you cannot hear him or anyone else screaming as they're knocked over and ripped apart by the rampaging ants.

"Hold on, just a moment," Murray squeaks. He rushes back to the wall, but he never reaches you. An ant

intercepts him, and squirts a clear liquid in his face. He screams, his face melting. Then he's torn apart.

The only person still fighting is Megan. She's holding off three ants with her laser lipstick. Maybe she can win? The overkill setting is definitely an advantage.

The Bugman sends more ants to attack her. Three giant-ant corpses are smoking on the floor when Megan is finally brought down.

"Megan!" you yell, but she doesn't move.

"She's dead," the scientist with the beard whispers.

The ants run toward you, and attack.

"Stop!" The Bugman yells, but not before the scientist with the beard has his head bitten off.

Smiling, the Bugman grabs Frankie with one arm and the remaining scientist with the other. "Don't move," he hisses. Then he gives a speech about the wonders of the World Wide Web of Evil.

It's time to make a decision. Do you:

Stand up for what you believe in? P46

Or

Tell the Bugman you want to join WOE? P50

Stand up for what you believe in

You walk up to the Bugman and say, “No, I’d rather die.”

“That’s easily arranged,” the Bugman says.

He points Frankie’s transmogrifier at the ceiling. He’s going to press the button!

You can’t stand around and watch, whatever plan the Bugman has, you’re sure it’ll be horrific. You grab his arm.

The machine backfires, and suddenly, the Bugman’s whole body ripples. He’s growing fur and shrinking at the same time. His nose becomes a pretty shade of pink and sprouts long whiskers – they wobble a little as he sniffs the air.

The Bugman has turned into a mouse?! Steve was right, but he was kind of wrong too. Frankie’s trans-mouse-ifier wasn’t silly, or all talk.

No time to worry about that. The mouse bunches up and jumps down onto the transmogrifier lying at your feet. Maybe he’s trying to push the buttons. You grab the mouse and place him in your pocket, before he can do any such thing.

"I would have gotten away with this," he squeaks. Then adds the terrible cliché, "If it wasn't for you meddling kids."

So not entirely a mouse then. A mouseman? Which isn't a bad name for the creature. You can hardly call him the Bugman anymore.

Frankie picks up her remote and points it at the remaining giant ants.

A balloon floats into the room. Frankie points her remote at it. There's a loud bang and Ms Xavier appears. "Not a word about Megan, or Murray, or Steve," she says stepping clear of shredded balloon. "I'm going to try and get them treatment."

"Treatment? But they're dead," the scientist says.

"Best to wait for a professional opinion, don't you think?" Ms Xavier says, calling in something called a World of Surgeons extraction unit.

As you leave the museum, you're swarmed by reporters and camera people. They all want to know your story, so you tell them some of the wildest tales they've ever heard. But you don't tell them about the Bugman, who is washing his whiskers in your pocket.

Everyone is impressed. Mostly because you tell them about how brave you were fighting off giant ants single handedly. Which isn't true. That was Megan. But you try not to think about her. Or Steve and Murray who fought so bravely against the Bugman's evil machinations. Hopefully

Ms Xavier can save them. Frankie and the remaining scientist exchange glances but they don't way a word either.

Having had more than a little fun making up stories, you decide to become a famous author and live in wealth and luxury. Sometimes you hear about strange organizations called WOE and WOS. According to the rumors, they're some kind of spy thing. But nobody believes such outrageous claims The stories that the silly Bugman was part of an evil group fighting against a clandestine spy agency, is even less likely than some of your books; A Day in the Life of the Mouseman, Attack of the Giant Bugs, and Saving the World a Day at a Time. In your autobiography, The Bugman and Me, you even admit the kids were playing spies, but they didn't know what they were doing any more than you.

Ms Xavier pops by sometimes to see how you are, and to tell you how well the others are going. But she's always racing off because, as you know, schoolteachers are the busiest people on earth. They have endless emergencies. And Ms Xavier has them more than most. Sometimes she's so worried about her students, you'd think she was saving the world or something.

After a few years, the Mouseman disappears, but he hasn't gone far. You can still hear his tiny voice plotting revenge from under the kitchen cupboard. Still, even though he was horrible, it can be lonely without him and

there are times when you're busy typing on your computer, or talking into your voice recorder, that you wonder what would have happened if you'd made a different choice.

Now you're an author you can find out. Whichever path you chose is going to be awesome fun, because there's nothing more exciting than a really good adventure. You might die horribly, then again you might even save the world – again.

For more adventure:

Go back to *Jeremy Wilder at the Museum?* P10

Or

Go to the Adventure Contents and choose any path. P184

Tell the Bugman you want to Join WOE

With your life on the line, you quickly decide to fall in line and join WOE. It is, after all, the only decision where you're likely to live.

"Excellent," the Bugman says. "I see we have no opposition. You're all going to do the prudent thing."

You nod eagerly. Surely that will keep the horrible man happy?

The Bugman smiles and nods.

"Thank goodness we're being sensible and doing the right thing," the scientist next to you whispers.

"Except," says the Bugman, "I've never liked suck-ups. So I've decided to feed you to the spiders after all. It's important work. I'm going to need plenty of spider silk over the next few days. I hope you're happy to know your contribution is going to be instrumental in allowing us to take over the world. Thank you all for joining the World of Evil, I hope you enjoy the last few minutes of your life." He points Frankie's transmogrifier at a spider web in the corner of the ceiling.

An enormous spider drops to the ground.

The Bugman searches through his pockets and sprays something at you, and the spider lunges. Enormous fangs the size of samurai swords sink into your chest.

You scream. But not for long. Everything goes black.

I'm sorry, you've been eaten. The world of bugs is a dangerous one, which is what makes it so exciting. There are many wonderfully horrible deaths, for someone brave enough to risk the Attack of the Giant Bugs.

There are also many wonderful opportunities. You could become one of the most famous inventors of all time and create inventions so amazing they'll take you up, past the stratosphere. Or you could become a super, top-secret spy and live a life full of extraordinary adventure. It's all up to you and the choices you make.

For more adventure, click on a link to:

Go back to *Jeremy Wilder at the Museum?* P10

Or

Go to the Adventure Contents and choose any path. P184

Stay with Steve and Defy the Bugman

You're standing right next to Steve as the Bugman looks at the strip of gum. He looks like he's about to take it, when an ant jumps to intercept, its jaws closing on the gum.

"Watch out!" Steve yells and pulls you back.

The gum explodes in a wave of sound and ant debris.

Your ears are ringing. Ant debris is everywhere. Gross.

You're just regaining your hearing when Steve yells, "Quick! Have you got your laser pen?"

Quickly, you pull out the pen Megan gave you and stand back-to-back with Steve. You're quickly surrounded. Steve is waving his laser pen, chopping ant limbs in half, but you're not doing so well, barely scorching them.

They're getting really close, jaws snapping in your face.

"Here, swap!" Steve yells, wheeling around to take care of another ant for you. He takes a moment to twiddle the settings and soon you're both chopping into the ants like Jedi Knights.

Megan and Murray are also swinging away with gusto. Soon all the ants are smoking corpses on the ground, their dismembered legs twitching.

The Bugman raises the transmogrifier.

"No!" Steve yells. He can't reach.

It's up to you. You have to grab it before the Bugman can push any buttons.

Diving, you snatch the transmogrifier from his hands, skid into a roll, and point it right back at him. The Bugman rushes to get back through the blackened hole in the wall, and you miss. The transmogrifier beam scorches the plaster even blacker before the Bugman crashes into it.

For a moment the Bugman's stuck, plaster and soot flying as he thrashes to get through the Steve-shaped hole. His haste only makes him slower, and there's just enough time for Steve and Megan to rush over to grab him and pull him away from the exit.

"But I wanted to take over the world. It was my destiny," The Buman yells. "And I would have gotten away with it if it wasn't for you rotten meddling kids."

"Indeed," comes a formal voice. Ms Xavier appears, climbing into the room without getting a speck of soot on her. Kennedy and the rest of her team are not far behind. After a short discussion with her students, Ms Xavier turns to you, "Well done. You've saved the world from the Bugman and his giant bugs. Have you thought about joining us at WOS – you know, the World of Spies. We could use quick thinkers like you."

That very afternoon you are brought to the WOS headquarters to receive a certificate that looks like a blank piece of paper, but that's only until you wave a black light over it while standing underneath a full moon.

Honorary WOS agent and Defeater of the most Evil of Villains, the Bugman.

Now you're an honorary member of the World of Spies, there are plenty of opportunities to help save the world again and again – and the added benefit of gaining access to heaps of spy gizmos like bullet-proof coats and umbrella swords. On one of the spy manuals there's a button, with the words, For adventure in fabulous locations, like trains, the buses, airplanes and even your own bedroom, join the WOS mailing list now. Also, a great opportunity to watch out for handy underground bunkers and discounts on books.

Despite your wonderful life, sometimes you wonder what life would be like if you'd made different choices. Well, Frankie's made a time machine, and she's offering you a chance to brave the dangerous world of bugs again. You never know what might happen. You might ride a butterfly, fight off a cockroach, or track down the Bugman using ant poop and explosives.

Well, this is your chance. Frankie's asking, would you like to:

Go back to *Jeremy Wilder at the Museum?* P10

Or

Go to the Adventure Contents and choose any path? P184

Volunteer to Help Kennedy Find Ms Xavier and Frankie

Some guy in painting overalls pushes a mop of dark hair off his face. He's wearing a nametag with Richard Palmer printed on it. "I'm coming with," he says in a Southern accent.

"I don't think so," Kennedy says. "Who are you anyway?"

"I was supposed to be one of today's instructors," he says, waving a piece of blank paper in Kennedy's face. "Although it might have been because Chief X thought I needed a bit more fieldwork before completing my undergrad spy certification. And now look where we are. I've been thrown into the deep end on a dangerous mission – with nothing but recruits."

"We'll be fine." Kennedy shakes her head, as if she knows she's lying. "Just don't think about it too hard." She hurries you both back out into the corridor. "Where should we start?" Kennedy shines her black-light on the piece of paper he's waving. A World of Stamp Collectors logo appears. It looks surprisingly similar to the World of Shoes sign that had been hanging on the door.

"This way," you say. You start walking back to the bug exhibit.

"Good idea, we'll track Ms Xavier from where you last saw her."

"Don't forget we're looking for someone small," you say.

Richard pulls out a pair of glasses. "These might be useful," he says. "Whatever happens, they'll keep me in touch with old Stevey-boy."

You hurry – not too fast – down the corridor, just in case Frankie's machine really could shrink someone. You've heard the stories that not all Frankie's machines work as advertised, and you don't want to run into it, or the Bugman.

You reach the last bug room. But there's still no one there – not even any bugs. That is, if you don't count the giant models. Determined, you start searching the rest of the museum. In the African room, a toddler in an elephant onesie is crying about their lost balloon.

"We'll help you find it," Kennedy says.

"Yeah, right." Richard smiles and nudges her. "Good excuse to look around."

Kennedy keeps looking behind exhibits. "It's not behind the stuffed rhino."

Richard looks in the open jaws of a stuffed alligator.

"It's not in here either. Impressive teeth though, especially with my super-vision glasses."

The toddler in the elephantsuit wanders away, disappointed.

"Okay," you say, stopping under a fake acacia tree. "We have to think. Where could she be hiding? We can't look in every exhibit this place has."

Something drops onto Kennedy's shoulder. "Get it off me," she yells. "It might be a Bugman bug."

It doesn't look like a bug. It looks like a miniature person. "Wait!" you shout.

"Yes, wait!" Richard yells. "It's Ms X. She's found us!"

You all put your ears as close to Ms Xavier as you dare, without crushing her.

"Stop dilly-dallying," she snaps. "We have to find that wretched girl, Frankie, before her invention gets us into even more trouble."

"What about using that balloon stuck in the branches?" Richard asks.

You look up. Sure enough, there's a red balloon above you, the string dangling over your heads. "Hey," you say, but the toddler's gone.

"Awesome," Richard says. "You're so little, Ms Xavier. You could use the helium balloon like a hot air balloon."

"Thank you for stating the obvious, Mr Palmer," says Ms Xavier. "What did you think I was doing up the tree?"

You hook the balloon down — and with the help of the others, you create a little basket out of bus timetables, advertising pamphlets and string. Kennedy pulls out her own dark glasses, takes a tiny black microphone from the bridge, and pins it to the edge of the basket. Then you carefully put Ms X inside.

The toddler's nowhere to be seen. Hopefully they won't mind too much.

"Don't worry, I'll find Frankie," Ms Xavier says.

Kennedy and Richard wave and say "Good luck, Ms X. Keep in touch."

"Now, where are we going?" Kennedy asks.

Do you:

Suggest you keep looking for Frankie? P61

Or

Suggest you follow the trail of the class and the Bugman? P80

Race up to Fight off the Ladybug with Your Laser Pen

The laser pen flares.

And that's it. It barely hurts the creature at all. Except for the nauseating smell of burnt hair, you wouldn't know it had been hit. Maybe the shell is slightly black where you singed it, but there's no other effect – except that the ladybug flies at you, mouth open, mandibles waving.

You feel the wind of the ladybug's wings, before you're grasped in its mandibles and sucked into its mouth.

In seconds, nothing is left except a shoe.

The real shame is that you were hardly a snack on the ladybug lunch menu and within moments all your friends will be dead, too. Still, the world of bugs is a dangerous one, which is what makes it so exciting. Next time when you head out on adventure you may like to die a hideous death, join the bad guys, or even save the world.

You wonder, in those last seconds as the memories of your life flash before your eyes, what would have happened

if you'd thrown the exploding chewing gum at the ladybug. Luckily, as the last dregs of your consciousness *fade, you can make a choice between three options:*

Go back in time and throw the exploding chewing gum. P41

Or

Go back to the beginning of the story. P6

Or

Go to the Adventure Contents and choose any path. P184

Suggest You Should Keep Looking for Frankie

"Good idea," says Kennedy. "When did someone last see her?"

"She was chasing after the tour guide, Jeremy Wilder," you say. "She hasn't been seen since he took her invention. Let's go back there."

"Awesome," Richard says.

You make your way through the exhibits, back to the Museum Staff Only door that Frankie and the tour guide went through.

On the other side is a corridor leading to a bunch of office cubicles. Old books line the shelves and there are many old posters featuring bugs and animals of all kinds. It's not a broom cupboard office, but it's still a lot dingier than the flash glass offices you see on TV.

An old lady asks why you're there. "You're not staff," she says.

"So sorry," Kennedy says, backing into the corridor. "We must be lost."

As you step backwards, you trip over something on the ground. A screwdriver. It skids across the floor. Frankie's screwdriver? A little further away is a scrap of paper.

You pick it up.

As soon as it's in your hand you realise it's not paper. Although it looks like paper, the texture is weird. It's almost spongy. Some kind of smart paper? Electronic? The message on it reads, He's going outside. There's a blinking arrow beside the message.

Do you:

Run outside? P63

Or

Press the arrow? P70

Run Outside

"Quick, let's go," you yell.

Kennedy and Richard follow you out the door, and stop. Outside, there's a small grass courtyard dotted with statues, elephants, famous people … that kind of thing. You look around for a bit, and are about to go back inside when you hear scuttling behind you.

The Bugman is right there, giant ants by his side.

"Nice of you to join me," he says. "Together, we can take over the world."

Do you:

Decide to join him (ant jaws are pretty ferocious)? P64

Or

Refuse the Bugman's offer? P66

Decide to Join Him

(ant jaws are pretty ferocious)

You smile as non-threateningly as you can at the Bugman, looking furtively at Kennedy and Richard. "Where do I sign up?"

"This way," the Bugman growls. He walks over to the statue of the elephant and lifts a trapdoor. "In you go," he orders.

He ant-walks you (it's like a perp walk, but with ants) and Kennedy and Richard to a small room at the end of the corridor, goes to his honeycomb-shaped drawers and pulls out a pile of paper. "How would you like life insurance?" he asks. "Double pay for extra time?"

Is he really offering you these things? "What?"

He cackles with laughter. "You fell for it. You think I'm going to pay you? That's hilarious. Alright minions, you're on kitchen duty for the first month. Anyone who doesn't work hard will be thrown to the spiders. Or the antlion. Or, well there are just so many choices. Hop to it."

He throws some sort of concoction into two of the ants' mouths, and they push you all the way to the kitchens,

where there are remarkably few knives and far too many enormous pots and dirty dishes.

There are a surprising number of humans willing to do the Bugman's bidding, now that he is the ruler of the world.

Your only hope is that someday, someone will return Mr Wilder's bugs back to their proper size.

Now your adventure is over, there are many paths to explore, including becoming a world class spy, a famous entomologist, or dying horribly in the tender embrace of a praying mantis.

Would you like to:

Start back at *Jeremy Wilder at the Museum?* P10

Or

Go to the Adventure Contents and choose any path? P184

Refuse the Bugman's Offer

The Bugman and his giant ants are blocking your way out of the courtyard. "My goodness, you are brave, aren't you?" He laughs. "Good, you'll be a snack for my ants."

Kennedy and Richard gulp, but they don't move. Nonchalantly, Kennedy pulls some chewing gum from her pocket. "Gum?" she says, holding up a packet of exploding gum to the Bugman.

"What? Oh, duck," Richard yells.

The Bugman backs off, so Kennedy throws a strip of gum at the two closest ants. One bounces off, but the other sticks. Then both strips explode with a kkkrrrumph that makes your ears ring.

Bits of one ant rain down.

The other ant's only slightly injured. It veers away from the smoking patch of dirt and rubble that used to be courtyard. You jump back, but you don't need to worry because three of its fellow ants jump on it and start eating.

You, Kennedy and Richard all run, but there's nowhere to go – the path is still blocked and the museum door can only be opened from the inside.

The Bugman laughs. "Mwah ha ha, you WOS trainees are pathetic."

WOS trainees?

All seems lost. But you stand by your companions. "Any ideas?" you ask.

Kennedy shakes her head. "It was a privilege to have known you. You would have made a great WOS operative. You know, World of Spies." She says it like it's the highest compliment she could ever give.

The ants are about to attack, when the ground opens up from under an elephant statue. A secret door? Under the elephant statue? Yes, really. You hadn't noticed, given there were other things to worry about – like staying alive.

Steve, Murray and Megan climb out with Frankie in tow. "You don't look like you're doing so well."

"Who said you could escape my secret lair?" the Bugman says. He points Frankie's machine at a bee flying over a dandelion. "Never mind. It doesn't matter. My amazing insects will take over the whole world, anyway. Did you really think you meddling kids could get in my way?"

The museum door opens and Ms Xavier appears. She's being towed on her balloon by two people wearing World of Safari shirts. The toddler in the elephant onesie is clutching the woman's shirt.

"You're even more pathetic than WOS agents," the Bugman says, preparing to point Frankie's transmogrifier at an anthill.

Seeing the danger, you dive at the Bugman, ignoring the enormous bee flying overhead.

The transmogrifier beam flashes.

Something screeches. It's a giant bird. "Hey, Ms Xavier, you're back," Richard yells. Then he starts screaming – snapped up by the giant bird.

You have to focus. You have to get the machine off the Bugman. He's remarkably strong, but Kennedy joins in and, between you, you manage to wrestle the machine off the Bugman. Quickly, you reverse the bird to normal size, and then start looking for other things to reverse, like the giant bee.

One of the WOS agents has been so traumatised that, even now that the bee's normal size, they're shrieking with fear. Frankie sighs. She carefully aims her remote and the bee transforms into a mouse.

Ms Xavier turns to you. "Congratulations, you have saved the world from the Bugman and his giant bugs." She invites you to the WOS headquarters where they shower you with praise. There's even a special certificate that looks like a piece of paper. When you wave a black light over it while underneath a full moon, it says, Hero of WOS and Honorary Member.

There's a big long boring speech, of course, but it's worth it. The best bit is being able to play with heaps of spy gizmos like laser pens and forget-me gum. (Always

useful when you've forgotten to do the dishes, or haven't handed your homework in on time.) There's even a special WOS mailing list you can join, if you sign up here. It's a great idea because everyone needs adventure, and there are so many real life events to escape like being bored on the train, the bus, an airplane and even Ms Xavier's next long boring lecture on integral calculus and real life applications.

Also, as an honorary member of the World of Spies, you have plenty of opportunities to help save the world again and again.

For more adventure, click on a link to:

Go back to *Jeremy Wilder at the Museum*. P10

Or

Go to the Adventure Contents and choose any path. P184

Press the Arrow

Another message comes up on Frankie's electronic paper. Elephant statue, left foot 23144 when 1 is from the front.

Kennedy, Richard and you crowd around puzzling over it.

"Great," Kennedy says. "Total gibberish."

"Well, we might as well go outside and look," Richard says. "Maybe there are statues out there."

You all agree, and traipse outside into the sunshine and onto a small lawn surrounded by statues.

There's an elephant statue right in front of you. It can't be a coincidence. "It must be a code," you say, examining Frankie's message paper again.

Elephant statue left foot 23144 when 1 is from the front.

"Awesome," says Richard. "It must be something to do with the toes on the elephant's left foot."

"Wait a minute." You look at the note. "Our left, or the elephant's left?"

Kennedy walks around the statue. "Look, the far toe has more damage."

"I'll bet that's the four," Richard says, but you guessed that already. Quickly, you press the toes in order. *Two, three, one, four, four.*

A hidden hatch opens with barely a creak.

It's so quiet in the courtyard, you can hear the muted thunk of someone pushing down the security bar on the other side of the museum door. It's opening.

"Quick," you whisper.

You all tumble through the hatch as fast as you can, slamming it behind you. Together, you run down the stairs and through the corridor, dimly lit with thin streaks of light sneaking out from under a few closed doors. Before you get far, you hear the sound of cursing from outside the hatch. "Blistering bugs! I always forget the code."

Kennedy puts on dark glasses, really dark glasses, and leads you confidently through the bunker. It seems weird that she's not running into walls.

"Ah, I think this is it!" Kennedy says as she leads you through an office with weird honeycomb-shaped drawers, and a bookcase full of spray cans. She opens the door into a large room lined with giant TV screens and strange machines with hundreds of buttons and switches. *My Evil Plan* is written in large friendly letters on the top of a whiteboard. Stuck to the whiteboard are clearly Photoshopped images of militarised insects taking over; brightly coloured peacock spiders are ushering in airplanes like they're air traffic control Marshalls (there's even a label that helpfully says peacock spiders), bees are swarming over City Hall, ants are parading down a main street where cars drive right through ants and vine-covered trees without crashing, and termites are creating a giant underground nest where the police department is. Nobody is running away in fear. People are still coming and going like it's a normal day. Finally, you notice the little letters at the bottom of the screens. *Simulation.*

"Why is it supervillains always skimp on post-production software?" Richard says.

"Come on," Kennedy says. "We don't have time. We have to stop this from happening. But how?"

You look at the strange machine. The buttons and switches must do something. "Maybe these control the insects," you say. They all have weird names like, *Roaches Revenge, Parachuting into Paris* and *Antwerp's Avaricious Ants.* Amongst the hundreds of buttons, switches and dials, two of the bigger buttons catch your attention.

A red button with the words, *The End Is Nigh.*

A green button with the words, *Happily Ever After.*

Giant ant footsteps echo from the corridor. "The Bugman's coming!" you whisper.

"We should press the green button now," Richard insists.

"Wait," Kennedy says. "I don't think saving the world is the Bugman's *happily ever after.*"

It's up to you to make the decision. Do you:

Press the red, *The End is Nigh,* button? P73
Or

Press the green, *Happily Ever After,* button? P77

Press the Red Button

You press the red button.

Nothing seems to happen, except the pungent smell of burning rubber rises from the machines.

A clock appears onscreen, and a computerised voice says, "Self-destruct in five minutes, and counting."

"Four minutes and 48 seconds, and counting."

"We need to get out of here!" Kennedy shouts.

"Stop, wait!" you yell. "There's only one way to get out of here and it's past the Bugman and his ants."

It's too late, Kennedy and Richard are already running.

Desperately, you scan the Bugman's office. There are hundreds of cans of spray. All different kinds. Ant-Bee-Good, Bugman Patented Spider Spray, Bugman Patented Bug Repellent, and more.

You pick up a can each of Ant-Bee-Good and Bugman Patented Bug Repellent. Soon you're running as fast as you can down the corridor yelling. "It's going to blow!"

The Bugman doesn't run away. He races toward you, and orders his ants to attack.

Richard and Kennedy have slowed, but you don't. You catch up to the others and run past, right at the ants

– spraying your cans in their faces while the countdown continues. "Four minutes and two seconds, and counting."

The ants shy away from the droplets and clack their mandibles. Are they confused or angry? Do insects even have emotions, or are they just waiting to kill you?

You spray again.

Then, as one, they attack the Bugman. Horrified, you watch as he's torn limb from limb.

Kennedy grabs you by the arm, and you hear the countdown again.

"Three minutes, and counting."

You look at each other and both yell, "Run!"

As you're racing for the exit, more and more people join you, some quite bewildered, others annoyed.

You're met by World of Spies agents, with dark, dark sunglasses and World of Spies clearly written on their vests. Some of the people wearing World Wide Web of Envelopes t-shirts try to run, but there's nowhere for them to go, and you're all quickly escorted to safety at the front of the museum. Waiting outside with his parents in World of Safari t-shirts is the toddler in the elephant onesie. The toddler and his parents wave at you.

You wave back, and as you do, you feel the rumble beneath your feet.

"Cover your head and duck," you yell to the kid. "It's going to explode!"

The ground is shaking with a rising growl.

Then, behind you, the museum explodes in a ball of flame and disappears into the ground.

Sirens arrive from everywhere. Cars unload police. And more police.

Many of the people from the underground lair are led away, and when you look around again, all the World of Spies agents have disappeared. Soon there's hardly anybody left except you, Kennedy and Richard – and people wearing various World of "Something" logos.

The parents of the toddler give you an elephant key-chain, with a single golden key attached. "This is the key to the zoo. Come and visit, if you ever need us."

The toddler waves goodbye. "Next time, I'll have lots of balloons. Mum said so."

Ms Xavier appears. "Congratulations, great work," she says. "You three stopped the Bugman. A bit unfortunate about the museum, but what can you do? Without your help we could have lost the whole city, even the world.

"We need people like you in WOS (World of Spies). Will you join Kennedy and Richard, tonight? We've decided to make you all fully-fledged field agents."

That night, when you are brought to the WOS head-quarters, they shower you with more praise, and give you a certificate that looks like a piece of paper and only shows your spy certification when you wave a black light over it underneath a full moon. You also receive a spy book with a button, advertising the WOS mailing list. If you join, you'll never know when or where you might find an adventure. Fabulous and exotic locations you can visit from the comfort of public transport or even your own bedroom. Also, watch out for underground bunkers and discounts on books. So Press this button now!

There's a big long boring speech, of course, but it's great because it means you're a field agent of the World of Spies. Now you can help save the world again and again, and even visit the zoo whenever you like. The best part is you get the most amazing spy gizmos, including a car that can be used as a submarine or an airplane with its own built-in defence and entertainment systems, and even a Frankie-patented limited-action time machine.

Sometimes, late at night, you wonder what would have happened if you didn't take this path. Would you have died in the merciless grip of a spider, or in the jaws of some other creepy crawly? Would you become a minion for the Bugman? Or found new and exciting ways to save the world?

For more adventure, click on a link to:

Go back to *Jeremy Wilder at the Museum.* P10

Or

Go to the Adventure Contents and choose any path. P184

Press the Green Button

A mass of balloons fall while triumphant music plays.

"What just happened?" Kennedy asks.

Richard shrugs.

The Bugman appears behind you, wearing his ridiculous grasshopper face-mask. "Congratulations, I was just about to press that button. Thank you for helping me take over the world."

"No!" you yell.

"Mwah ha ha. Hold them!" he snaps to the ants.

The ants grab you with their mandibles (insect mouths that look like pincers lined with teeth).

It's terrible. The more you struggle, the more the mandibles bite into you. You're unable to do anything but watch. He presses more buttons on the enormous control board. A tray opens, and he shoves Frankie's machine into the hatch labelled SuperSize.

On the screens, people are no longer walking through the giant insects, they're screaming and running away in terror. It's no longer a simulation. Giant bees are really swarming over City Hall. Giant spiders are really falling from the sky on enormous parachutes. Ants are parading down Main Street. Termites are creating a massive mound outside the police station. The longer you look, the more horrible it is.

"Mwah ha ha," the Bugman says. "See my giant spiders? Aren't they magnificent? Soon they'll be running all the airports and parachuting into every major city in the world."

The Bugman has weaponised Frankie's machine! And now he's about to take over the world.

What an evil diabolical genius.

He's already turning his monitors to more simulations. Huge insects are taking over the White House and hundreds of parliamentary buildings all around the world. Even Buckingham palace!

The world is at risk! The madman is destroying everything! You struggle valiantly. Kennedy and Richard are crying out in horror, pleading for the Bugman to change his mind.

All your struggling is futile. The ant jaws grip you tighter and tighter.

"Oh, go feed them to your young," is the last thing you hear before the ants tear you apart.

I'm sorry, you've been eaten. The world of bugs is a dangerous one, and the world of evil villains, even more dangerous. Sometimes a single decision can mean life or

death. If you want to find out what would have happened if you pressed the big red button, why not try now? If not, there are still more adventures, more gloriously hideous deaths, and opportunities – not just to become a heroic super-spy, but to join the bad guys, or be turned into a mouse!

For more adventure, click on a link to:

Go back to *Jeremy Wilder at the Museum*. P10

Or

Go to the Adventure Contents and choose any path. P184

Suggest You Follow the Trail of the Class and the Bugman

Kennedy and Richard agree, and you all hurry back to the bug exhibit.

You look around. The class is gone! The terrariums are gone! There's nothing left except the giant models and displays.

"What's this?" Kennedy asks, kicking brown scat across the floor.

"Ant poop!" Richard says.

You follow the trail of giant ant poop through a door and out to a grassy courtyard surrounded by statues. The trail stops at the base of an elephant statue.

There are other statues around, but nothing else that catches your eye.

Where could they have gone? Under the statue? Maybe they shrank? Or have you lost the trail? Where else could the ants have gone?

You retrace your steps, intending to go back into the museum to get help, but the door is firmly locked. You skirt

around the outside of the building along a narrow path. No sign of ants yet. But there's a lot of noise coming from the front of the museum.

"Maybe the ant poop trail really did lead to a hideout under the elephant statue," you say.

Kennedy shrugs. "Better check that racket first." She holds up an arm and together you creep very slowly around the side of the building.

As you approach, you see the commotion is from people protesting behind police tape. Journalists are busy shoving microphones in people's faces and emergency services are all there, lights swirling, but without their sirens. Out, beyond the crowd, smoke from fires hangs over the city, and there's the distant wail of sirens punctuated by the crack of gunshots.

The city's in chaos.

With all these police about, maybe they can help. Relieved, you step out from the shadows.

The ominous click of guns greets you. Police are pointing their guns at the three of you!

A loudspeaker squawks so loudly you want to clap your hands over your ears, but moving doesn't seem like a good idea.

The loudspeaker roars into life. "Stay where you are and put your hands up!"

Kennedy, Richard and you put up your hands – very slowly.

The police don't move, as if they're not sure what to do.

"I don't like this," Kennedy whispers.

"Join the club," Richard mutters.

You try not to laugh. Maybe it was the bad joke, or maybe it's the toddler in the elephant onesie running out fearlessly in front of the police. "Don't shoot, they're my fwends. Look! I got my bawoon back. See? It's a got a basket and a tiny person."

Two people with World of Safari shirts dash over to the toddler. "That's okay, darling," the woman says and they hurry him away. But nobody seems too frightened of you anymore.

Three journalists rush over. They thrust microphones into your faces. "What is happening? Who's taking over the world? Is there anything you'd like to say?"

Kennedy and Richard are silent. Kennedy's too busy texting something on her phone, probably letting people know where Ms Xavier is. And Richard is looking in the wrong direction.

You have to say something. Do you:

Tell the journalists the Bugman has a hideout under the elephant statue. P83

Or

Tell the journalists you're just a kid on a school trip. P86

Tell the Journalists the Bugman has a Hideout under the Elephant Statue

"It would make sense," Kennedy says. "There's nowhere else the giant ants and all those people could have gone."

Two police officers in freshly starched uniforms step forward. "Show us," they say.

You, Kennedy and Richard lead them to the elephant statue. The trail of ant-poop clearly ends here. "See?" You point.

One of them sneers. "This is ridiculous! Why are we listening to kids blathering about ant poop?"

"Fine," Kennedy says. "Stand back." She pulls two whole packets of gum from her pocket and throws them in front of the statue.

The earth explodes. You try to duck, but fall over as the ground rocks beneath your feet. When you get up again, everyone's covered in dirt and grass.

Red-faced, the police brush the mess off their uniforMs They turn on Kennedy, "Your mother will hear about this! What has she said about you carrying explosives?"

Kennedy shrugs and points at the hole.

You peer into the murk. There's a secret passage below, with two very singed, giant ant carcasses. They smell disgusting, like burnt hair – and they're still smoking. It's so revolting you almost vomit.

The sneery police officer does vomit.

Kennedy laughs. "Come on," she says. "Let's have a look. Maybe we can—"

"Oh no, you don't," one of the officers mutters. Then they both try to shoo you away.

There's a countdown running. "Four minutes and 48 seconds and counting." It's coming from inside the bunker.

"Blast," Kennedy yells. "I think someone's activated a self-destruct."

"A bomb!" you shout. "We have to get everybody out of there!"

"Go and get a rope," Kennedy yells at the police. She jumps into the ragged hole, squeezing past the giant ant corpses and into a segment of corridor only partially filled with rubble and dirt. You and Richard follow her.

The stinking ant carcasses smell worse from down here. You look around. World of Evil posters tenaciously cling to

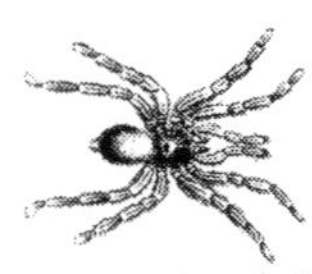

the walls, but each of the exits are blocked with piles of dirt and rubble.

Muffled voices and desperate scrabbling comes from behind one of the piles of rubble.

"Four minutes and ten seconds and counting."

Together, you start clearing the boulders. Soon the police have found a ladder and there's a chain gang removing the rubble.

"One minute and counting."

You hear Frankie' voice on the other side. "I can stop the bomb without the code," she says. "I can solve it, but only if someone can tell me what the Bugman's favorite insects are. One has 11 letters. The other has three."

She gives you three choices.

Ant. Grasshopper.

Or

Bee. Caterpillar.

Or

Cat. Lepidoptera.

Tell the Journalists You're just a Kid on a School Trip

Some friendly people pull you, Kennedy and Richard through the crowd at the front of the museum, toward a waiting ambulance. A lady in a pink dress hands you a hot chocolate, and the paramedics give you a blanket for the shock.

"I'm in shock. Look, I've got a blanket," Kennedy jokes.

Not that the blankets and hot chocolate make you feel any better. In less than an hour, the news is released that the Bugman has taken over the world. You, and everyone in the whole world are now his minions. Your only hope is that someday, someone will return Mr Wilder's bugs back to their proper size.

Now your adventure is over, there are so many paths to explore; becoming a world class spy, raising your own dragons, or even dying horribly while being torn apart by ants.

For more adventure, click on a link to:

Go back to *Jeremy Wilder at the Museum.* P10
Or

Go to the Adventure Contents and choose any path. P184

Follow Frankie Through the Staff Only Door

You run as fast as you can, to catch up to Frankie, and crash into a glass cage filled with monarch butterflies. They flutter into the air. The plaque on the butterfly cage says, Most butterflies feed on nectar. Our feeder contains fortified sugar water.

You've lost sight of Frankie. Where is she? Oh, there she is, disappearing around a corner. You run to follow and crash into her. Ow! She holds her finger to her lips, and points to something.

It's the tour guide, Jeremy Wilder, putting on an ugly grasshopper mask. Turning, he spots you and Frankie.

"Mwah ha ha," he says. "Two kids can't stop me. I'm the Bugman and I'm going to take over the world." He points Frankie's transmogrification remote at the two of you.

Do you:

Try and grab the remote? P88

Or

Put your hands up? P93

Try to Grab the Remote

Bravely, you rush over and grab at Frankie's remote. You get your fingers on it, but the Bugman isn't giving up without a fight. Frankie runs up to help.

The Bugman steps back, pulling at the remote. He's trying to yank it free.

You hold on tight, even though he's dragging you like you're on the losing side of a tug of war. For a skinny guy, he's pretty strong.

Beep.

"Oh, no!" says Frankie. "What are you doing with my transmogrifier?"

A spider on the ceiling grows to an enormous size. It drops to the floor, all its eight eyes watching you.

"Quick, hit the reverse button for exactly two seconds," Frankie yells. "It's the black one."

You struggle, stretching your thumb to hit the black button while the Bugman is fighting you for Frankie's machine.

It buzzes. There's more beeping. Beep, beep, BEEEEEP. The machine's vibrating so fast, it's hard to hold on.

"It's going to explode!" Frankie yells.

You let go.

The Bugman opens the door. He throws the machine into a room full of terrariuMs Full of bugs.

Frankie's machine explodes in a flash of light. In seconds, all the bugs in the room are growing.

There are ants as big bulldogs, scorpions the size of lions, and a praying mantis that towers over everything (fortunately there's a really high ceiling). A moth grows so big it breaks out of its container, showering shimmering wing-scales everywhere. And there's a monarch butterfly as large as a pony – no, a horse. It flies up and lands on a display table, the glass cracking under its feet.

It's so beautiful you watch, entranced, as it lifts up again in a shower of falling glass. It flies toward you.

"What's that?" Frankie yells, pointing.

You turn. A long hairy leg is poking around the door.

The Bugman claps his excitement. He walks right up to you and Frankie, laughing an artificial mwah ha ha ha laugh, like he's practiced being a supervillain.

The creature with the hairy leg rounds the corner – it's a tarantula spider! Its fangs drip poison. Surely you're going to die. The spider's fangs rise higher still, much to the amusement of the Bugman, who sprays something at the spider. "Mwah ha ha, now do my bidding and kill these fools."

The spider rears up.

You and Frankie run.

There's a harrowing scream behind you. It's the Bugman. The spider is paralyzing him with venom. His final words are, "Rats, I should have used my Bugman Patented Spider Spray, not the—"

Ants, spiders, bees, praying mantises, cockroaches, and butterflies all swarm out of the room. Some of them start to organise. One of them picks up Frankie's machine and points it at a terrarium just outside the door.

What? Thinking bugs? What was that spray the Bugman used? You run and keep on running. There's nothing you can do as police, and even the army rush in to combat the giant insects. But they're large, they're organised, and they're creating more over-sized creepy-crawlies all the time.

That evening you watch the news as it shows planes being flagged down by peacock spiders as they dance a waggly dance, bees taking over city hall, and ants making a giant nest and declaring themselves Supreme Rulers. The news lady reports that the ants are using Morse code to communicate with the creatures they call, the Primitive Mammals. And that she's been instructed that from now on she must use the words primitive mammals when talking about humans.

A lot of people die at the hands (mandibles, if you prefer) of the new insect rulers before anyone stops to think about why the ants are bright enough to use Morse code. You're sure it has something to do with the Bugman's spray. And there's a rumor that they've gathered scientists from all over the world – including Frankie – and locked them into a room with instructions to replicate the Bugman's spray. You hope they never do. And that one day you'll be free from this dreadful bug tyranny.

As a slave, you have to look after the ants' young all the time. And there's nothing worse than looking after spoilt children, except for looking after spoilt children who will eat you if you don't feed them fast enough. And then, very sadly, one day before the planned revolution, a hungry worker ant grabs you by the feet and eats you alive.

With your final breath you wonder what would have happened if you'd made different decisions. Maybe you could have become a famous world-class spy?

Postscript:

It may seem strange, but six months after your death Frankie manages to reverse the polarity of the transmogrifier, and reduces the insects back to normal size. Her first action as leader of the resistance is to immortalise your efforts to stop the Bugman. As a hero of the resistance, a statue of you is placed inside the courtyard of the new World of Spies headquarters.

Still, being honored when you are dead is sad as you don't get to enjoy it like you would if you were alive.

Next time you brave adventure, and possible glory, you could ride a butterfly, press the button that will either destroy or save the world, or play with secret codes and spy gizmos. You could even defeat the Bugman yourself.

For more adventure, click on a link to:

Go back to *Jeremy Wilder at the Museum*. P10

Or

Go to the Adventure Contents and choose any path. P184

Put Your Hands Up

"Congratulations," the Bugman says, grinning at Frankie. "It seems only fitting that I should test this device on you first."

He points the transmogrification machine at both of you.

"No," Frankie yells. She moves to jump in front of you, but before you know it, you've both been shrunk.

"Brilliant!" the Bugman says. "Better than my wildest dreaMs My insects and I shall take over the entire world and turn it into my personal paradise." Laughing, he picks you up in a hand that has finger nails bigger than you are. "Now, where shall I put you?"

"Turn us back to our proper size, now!" Frankie yells. You yell, too. But that only makes the Bugman laugh harder, his voice thundering in your ears. He goes to a terrarium and releases most of a colony of ants onto the floor. Then, he drops you in.

"Look at this," he says, cackling as he sprays a can of Bugman Patented Ant-Bee-Good spray over the ants and then points the remote at them.

Immediately, they become huge. It's hard to tell, because you're so small, but they must be as large as

Rottweilers, because they reach the Bugman's thighs. They march down the corridor after him. "See how they obey me – first Greenville, and then the world."

"One minute!" you hear him yell. "Forgot something." He comes back into the room, randomly waving Frankie's transmogrifier at terrariums full of clothes moths, monarch butterflies, scorpions, and a praying mantis. "Mwah ha ha ha," he says and runs out the door screaming with laughter as giant insects break out of their terrariuMs

Some of them follow him, others wander around the room.

"Are we going to escape?" Frankie asks. "Or do you think we should wait until we're rescued?"

"No," you say. "There's no time. Someone has to try and save Greenville from those giant bugs."

"But even if we could reverse the shrinking, we'd still be eaten by some of the giant insects out there. Look how dangerous they are." She points outside the glass terrarium to a human-sized praying mantis eating the head off a giant cockroach.

"What do we have?" you ask. "We can't just give up." You both go through your pockets. You have some coins and a piece of fluff. Not much use. But Frankie's pockets are stuffed to bursting. She has a mini screwdriver, a boiled sweet, a piece of string, and a sugar packet. She shrugs. "Never know when you're going to need sugar," she says.

"It's great for rocket fuel."

There's a sound of wind rushing under enormous wings. You look up. It's a giant butterfly, circling the terrarium. Then you realise, it's an ordinary-sized butterfly, but you're very small. So it just looks giant, especially this close. You also remember the plaque on the butterfly cage said butterflies will eat sugar water. Maybe you could entice it with some. Surely it's big enough to fly you out of here. "Hey Frankie, if we put the sugar in the water bowl, the giant butterfly might come down to feed."

"Great work, brainbox," Frankie says.

Before you can do anything, something shiny scuttles toward you. It's an enormous ant with jaws as big as you are. Well, it's a normal sized ant, but it's giant compared to you. It snaps its jaws.

Do you:

Race over to add the sugar to the water bowl? P96

Or

Attack the ant with Frankie's mini screwdriver? P122

Race Over to Add Sugar to the Water Bowl

There's not much time – the ant is right behind you. You run and jump up onto the edge of the bowl.

"Quick," Frankie yells, waving the screwdriver at the ant. "Dump the sugar packet."

You pull the packet open. It's about the same size as the palm of your hand.

The sugar tumbles into the water as the ant veers away from Frankie. It's heading toward you, then it flinches back, feelers waving.

A flurry of wind batters you from above. The butterfly lands, its long proboscis unfurling to suck in the sugar water.

The ant slinks closer.

Together, you and Frankie jump onto the fuzzy brown fur on the butterfly's back. Frankie is wielding the mini-screwdriver to keep the ant at bay.

The butterfly, finally noticing the danger, flinches away from the ant. It rolls its proboscis back up like a curly straw.

Wings unfurl to either side.

You hold on tight. Frankie does to. She can no longer reach the ant as it launches an attack on the butterfly's flank.

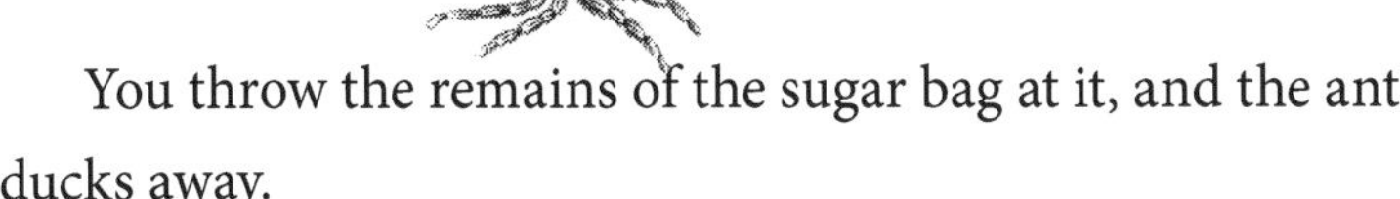

You throw the remains of the sugar bag at it, and the ant ducks away.

There's a whoosh, a flurry of wings, and you're in the air. The last you see of the ant is its open jaws. Then you're flying over the heads of even bigger and more dangerous insects, holding on tighter than ever. It's like riding a wild bull, or a very rough ocean as you bob up and down with each wingbeat.

You're just getting used to it when the butterfly takes you through an open door.

"What do we do now?" Frankie asks. "How are we going to get the transmogrifier so we can get back to normal? I don't want to be this size forever!"

"Forever!"

Somehow, you have to control the butterfly and get the remote back, but all you can do is hold on tight as the butterfly swings around a table.

The Bugman is below. You can tell it's him, even though he's so big, because of the huge green mask.

"There he is!" you yell. "He's racing out that exit with all his giant ants."

"Quick, help me throw the string around the butterfly," Frankie yells. "We can make it into reins!"

Do you:

Help Frankie use the string as reins? P98
Or
Tell Frankie you don't want to risk hurting the butterfly.

Help Frankie use the String as Reins

Frankie ties a boiled sweet to the end of the string to weight it. "Ready to catch," she yells. "Three, two one!" She throws the boiled sweet so the string swings around the butterfly's neck. You catch it.

Frankie grins at you. "Quick!" she says. "Pull. We need to fly that way, toward the giant ants."

You pull on the reins. The butterfly shakes and bucks. It's clearly upset. But it's turning to fly in the direction you want.

Do you:

Keep pulling on the butterfly reins.
Or
Tell Frankie to stop pulling on the butterfly reins.

Keep Pulling on the Butterfly Reins

You pull the butterfly back on course.

"Eureka," Frankie yells. "Let's get that invention-stealing, monster-ant creating— Aargh!"

The butterfly dives. It twists and turns.

"Get it back on track," Frankie yells. "Pull!"

"I'm trying," you yell back, holding onto the reigns for dear life.

The butterfly rolls upside down.

Frankie falls, screaming.

The tension on the string gone – you topple after her, still clinging to the boiled sweet. The ground is coming up fast – a terrarium filled with dirt, plants and a giant bowl of petunias.

Crunch! Your arm explodes in pain.

Bone is sticking out of your shin. There's blood, a lot of it. Frankie rips a piece of cloth from her sleeve and tries to staunch the bleeding. "I'll make a splint," she says. "Just a micro-second. I need to find a bit of wood, or something."

A round piece of ground flips up, like a very well camouflaged trapdoor. Normally, it'd be about the size of a large coin, but now you're tiny, it's bigger than you are.

Two brown hairy legs come out.

With your broken leg, you can't outrun whatever is emerging from that trapdoor. One by one, more legs appear, until you can see that this monster is a spider with eight long hairy legs, and enormous fangs.

It moves fast. First, it looks like it's going after Frankie, but as soon as she's out of sight, it reverses and scuttles toward you.

In a blur of motion, it grabs you with its front legs and sinks it's fangs into your shoulder.

Pain explodes. You scream, and try to struggle, but you're paralyzed.

The creature drags you to a dark hole in the ground.

You look out in the hope of seeing Frankie, but all you can see are the words, Oh, no, not again, painted in large friendly letters on the bowl of petunias, before the trapdoor shuts.

There is only endless darkness as you're slowly eaten alive.

I'm sorry, you've been eaten. The world of bugs is very exciting, and very, very dangerous. Next time when you head out on adventure, you could find another concealed

trapdoor, fight a giant ladybug, join the bad guys, or even take better care of the butterfly.

As the last synapse in your brain fires, you wonder what would have happened if you'd made different choices. An image of Frankie fills your mind. "Quick," she says. "We can rewrite history. I need to know—

"Do you want to:

"Go back to *Jeremy Wilder at the Museum?* P10

"Or

"Go back in time and stop using the reins on the butterfly?" P102

Tell Frankie to Stop Pulling on the Butterfly Reins

"He's getting away!" Frankie yells, pointing at the Bugman.

"You're the genius!" you yell back. "Think of something. And before he goes through that door."

"Oh yeah. Wait a minute. How do people get horses to change direction without reins?"

"They pull their mane, or use their legs? If we pull on the butterfly fur it might work."

"Okay, pull gently when I call right. Right."

You pull.

The butterfly turns right.

"Perfect," Frankie yells. "Let me try now."

You relax and the butterfly turns left.

Between the two of you, you steer the butterfly through the doorway and over the heads of the giant insects and people below. The feeling is exhilarating, and scary. You have to remind yourself not to get caught up in the feeling of flying or worry too much about falling.

Frankie yells, "Quick, he's just to the right. We almost have him!"

You pull on the butterfly's fur. It swings right. You're almost on top of the Bugman when Frankie yells, "Ease off, now!" but he doesn't even look, he just keeps striding toward a lot of giant heads, his giant insects in tow.

You check out the giant heads, they look really weird, but kind of familiar. "Oh no, that's our classes!"

"Hands up," the Bugman says, waving the remote at Ms Xavier.

Ms Xavier stands up. "Stay away from my class, and stop waving that silly machine."

A beam of light erupts from Frankie's transmogrifier.

Ms Xavier is now as small as you. Tiny as she is, she doesn't back away.

The class screams. Everyone breaks into a run.

The butterfly veers away from the commotion.

"Malfunctioning mechanisms!" Frankie yells. Beneath you, giant ants block the doors, jaws snapping.

"Stop!" The Bugman waves the transmogrifier. "Or I'll feed you all to my giant ants. Or something much worse."

As he rounds up the frightened students, you whisper to Frankie, "Where's Kennedy?"

"She's probably sneaking off to the spies meeting," Frankie says nonchalantly.

"Wait! What?"

"Don't worry about the World of Spies right now," Frankie says. "We have to save Ms Xavier before she's eaten by that cockroach. See it sniffing her out?"

A brown, shiny-armored monster scuttles toward the tiny Ms Xavier, woggling its antennae. A cockroach!

You pull the butterfly fur, angling carefully so the butterfly spirals down.

"Ms Xavier!" you yell. "Watch out for the cockroach." You drop the end of the string down to her, and steady the butterfly. Ms Xavier grabs the string and climbs onto the butterfly's back. By the time she's reached you, you're dizzy from all the circling.

"Quick, we have to follow the Bugman," Ms, Xavier says. "We need to get that dangerous invention of Frankie's back before it causes any more trouble."

Together, the three of you fly closer and closer to the Bugman, until you're just hovering over his head again. Below, you spy Frankie's transmogrifier sticking out of his trouser pocket. "Let me down," Ms Xavier says. "I'm going to climb down and get that infernal transmogrifier. Hold on tight."

You and Frankie hold tight to Frankie's string while Ms Xavier slides down. She drops onto the Bugman's head.

It's time to make a decision. Do you:

Chase after Ms Xavier to get the remote back? P105

Or

Stay on the Butterfly's back and distract the Bugman? P116

Chase After Ms Xavier to Get the Remote Back

"Hold on tight," you yell to Frankie as you clamber hand over hand down the string after Ms Xavier. Swinging on that string is like waiting to skydive, but you don't have a parachute and your hands are burning. And falling is not an option.

"Blue is big, pink is petite," Frankie yells down after you.

"Got it," you yell back, swinging yourself over the Bugman's head. Catching onto a strand of his hair, you jump down and swing over to Ms Xavier.

Above, Frankie and the butterfly are still circling.

"Hey!" the Bugman cries out, swatting at the butterfly. One of his giant ants snaps its jaws.

While they're distracted, you and Ms Xavier scramble down to where Frankie's remote is sticking out of the Bugman's pocket.

There are three enormous buttons. One is black, one is pink and the other has lost a sticker and is gray, the same as

the rest of the remote. Which button do you press, the black or the gray button? (Obviously, not the pink button. You're small enough already!)

Do you:

Press the black button and jump in front of the transmogrifier? P107

Or

Press the gray button and jump in front of the transmogrifier? P111

PRESS THE BLACK BUTTON AND JUMP IN FRONT OF THE TRANSMOGRIFIER

Whoosh. Everything changes all at once, your vision spins as the world seems to shrink. Frankie jumps from the butterfly, and dive rolls onto the floor, getting bigger by the moment. The butterfly wings away, evading Frankie's outstretched arm. A shrinking ant snaps its jaws at both of them, before it shrinks further and runs away.

Phew. Everything's back to normal. The Bugman's giant ants are small. You and Ms Xavier are normal size. The class is waving at you, half of them from behind their cellphones. You wave back.

"Oh, dear," Frankie points at the Bugman. "Did you press the black button? I think he's turning a mouse."

The Bugman's mask has fallen off to make way for growing whiskers and a pink wobbly nose. It's weird watching him change. Hands turning into paws, he scrubs at the fur growing on his face. Then his legs buckle and he shrinks, leaving his clothes in a puddle on the floor. He washes his whiskers, a knowing look in his eye.

Ms Xavier scoops up the mouse. “You’re going to pay for this, Bugman, or should I say, Bug-mouse?”

“Mwah ha ha, eek,” the Bugmouse laughs. “Look how cute I am. No one will ever believe you.”

“That’s funny,” Frankie says. “Haven’t you noticed?”

Half a dozen students wave their cellphones. “Best invention ever, Frankie.”

“Still.” Frankie sighs. “I guess, I’d better get you back to proper size. Where’s my transmogrifier?”

You spy it on the floor. It must have dropped it from the Bugman’s pocket when you hit the button. “Here. But shouldn’t we wait before we change him back?”

“Good idea,” says Ms Xavier. She puts the Bug-mouse in her pocket. “He’ll be safe in here while we wait for the police.” She puts her finger to her ear, like she’s wearing an earpiece. “They’ll be here any second. Three. Two. One—”

The police burst in the door. They look about.

“No need for theatrics,” Ms Xavier says. “Everything is under control.”

The police look confused. Some of the class try and explain what happened, others show the officers pictures and videos on their phones.

While they’re all distracted, Ms Xavier pulls you and Frankie aside. “Would you like to be part of the World of Spies? WOS is a great organization. We look after the planet and go on exciting missions, heroically saving people from

the World Wide Web of Evil."

Frankie looks at Ms Xavier. "I've already told you, no. My research is too important to be owned by a secret group. Just like Tesla, my inventions need to be in the public domain."

"That's fine," says Ms Xavier. "But how about you?" She looks right at you. "Have you thought about all the opportunities WOS can offer?"

Frankie shakes her head at you.

"Um," you say. "Maybe another day."

When everything is cleared up, Frankie takes you aside. "How about you join my team? We can be world-famous inventors together."

"But I haven't invented anything," you reply.

"Yes, I know, but you can think on your feet, and besides, I need someone to tell me what not to invent. Like the butterfly reins. I'm sure you'll get the hang of it."

And sure enough, you do. Together, you and Frankie become the most famous inventors of all time. You invent a time machine that runs on clean energy and solar airplanes that fly anywhere in the world in under thirty minutes.

WOS is always trying to get you to join them, but inventing things is too exciting. It's monsters one day and physics the next – besides, you never want to miss out on any of the Mars missions: they're too much fun. The Martians are hilarious.

Congratulations on your success, this story is over, but there are so many more. You can watch as bugs destroy the world, or you can save the museum from being blown up. A hero or a villain, it's all the same to some people – but is it the same to you?

For more adventure, click on a link to:

Go back to *Jeremy Wilder at the Museum*. P10

Or

Go to the Adventure Contents and choose any path. P184

Press the Gray Button and Jump in Front of the Transmogrifier

Whoosh. You start to fall, the world swirling dizzyingly around you. Everything's getting smaller – no, you're getting bigger –

You're about to hit the ground – you throw out your arms—

Thud.

"Ow." Your hand explodes in pain, but it doesn't appear broken. When you look up, everything is back to normal size. No, not everything. The ants are still huge. And Frankie. She's still tiny, and clinging onto the back of the butterfly for dear life.

Ms Xavier grabs the Bugman in an arm lock. One of the giant ants bites her leg.

"You're going to pay for this, Jeremy," Ms Xavier says through gritted teeth.

"I'm the Bugman," he yells, and grabs for Frankie's transmogrifier with his free hand. But you're too fast. You snatch the machine from his pocket before he can reach it.

"You think you can stop me?!" he yells. "Ants attack!"

You laugh. He's too late. Turning, you point the transmogrifier at the closest ant and press the pink button. One ant, two ants, three ants – soon they're all back to normal size.

"Thank you," Ms Xavier says.

There's no time to celebrate, the butterfly is fluttering away. You need to save Frankie. You reach up, aim the transmogrifier at Frankie and press the gray button again.

Wooosh.

Oops – the butterfly grows to the size of a kitchen table. Frankie's still holding tight to its back. At least she's normal size again.

There's a rush of air as the giant butterfly wings toward you.

You duck, and so does everybody else. Someone is screaming.

Sirens blare over the noise and two cops burst in, guns drawn.

"Don't shoot," you yell. "Butterflies only eat nectar or sugar water. Besides, Frankie's on that butterfly."

"Oh, yeah. Man, she's really done it this time."

"Hey," Frankie says. She leaps down from the butterfly. "It's not that bad." You hand the transmogrifier to her and she points it at the butterfly. "Bye," she says, pressing the pink button.

The butterfly shrinks and flutters away.

"Frankie, I really wish you wouldn't," a policewoman says.

"Wow," her partner says. "My first day out in the field and I've had to face mutant killer butterflies."

"Hardly killer," Frankie mutters. "Or mutant."

"It's always something, isn't it, Frankie?" The policewoman folds her arms.

"Hey." Kennedy appears and throws her arms around the woman. Where had Kennedy gone anyway, and why was she hugging a cop?"

"Stop fussing, Mom," Kennedy says.

Oh.

"Been busy, Kennedy?" her mom asked.

"Not so much," Kennedy says. "Looks like Ms Xavier, and my amazing best friend here, saved the day today." She nods at you.

"All in a day's work," Ms Xavier says. She takes the transmogrifier off Frankie and puts it in her pocket.

"Hey!" Frankie says.

"That's enough, Frankie. You know your inventions are too dangerous for the classroom. And far too dangerous for field trips. Still, if you join us at WOS, the World of Spies, you might get it back."

"No."

Ms Xavier taps her ear. "I'm afraid I can't take no for an answer."

"Fine," Frankie harrumphs. "As long as my new friend joins too."

Ms Xavier turns to you. "Well done, you've saved the day, your class, all Greenville, possibly the world. Who knows how much trouble giant bugs could have been? but now I'm going to offer you the opportunity of a lifetime."

"Make sure there's a party," Kennedy prompts.

You look over at Ms Xavier.

"Great idea." Before you know it, you're whisked off to the WOS headquarters. Half Ms Xavier's class is there. They shower you with praise, and give you a certificate that looks like a piece of paper until you wave it under a black light on a night with a full moon. Ms Xavier makes a big long boring speech, but nobody's listening, they've already started on the cake and lemonade.

"Congratulations," Ms Xavier says. "You are now an honorary member of the World of Spies. It's now your duty to save the world again and again, until you either die horribly or retire to a tropical island with your favorite book and a two hundred year supply of marmalade."

Now you're a WOS member you can press this button and join the WOS mailing list. You never know when or where you might find an adventure. Fabulous locations beckon – like the train, the bus, airplanes and even your favorite chair. Also it's important to watch out for underground bunkers and discounts on books. But in the

meantime, there are many more amazing adventures to be had. You could become a world-famous cheesemaker, an exceptional inventor, or become a minion for the Bugman and be forced to look after his baby army ants.

For more adventure, click on a link to:

Go back to *Jeremy Wilder at the Museum*. P10

Or

Go to the Adventure Contents and choose any path. P184

Stay on the Butterfly's Back to Distract the Bugman

Once Frankie and Ms Xavier drop down onto the Bugman's head, you coil up the string again and coax the butterfly into the villain's line of sight.

Your distraction works. The Bugman growls at you, grabs the remote from his pocket, aims it at you.

The beam from the transmogrifier leaves a scorch-mark on the ceiling.

You bring the butterfly around again.

"Mwah ha ha ha," his laugh booms out, louder than a rock band on full volume. You lean in, low on the butterfly's back, struggling to hold on. The butterfly whirls crazily, avoiding the flashing light as the Bugman takes multiple shots at you, scorching the ceiling.

Another flash. He's hit a spider.

It drops, growing to the size of a miniature pony, before it hits the ground and races toward him, fangs raised.

Quick! You have to rescue Frankie and Ms Xavier.

Frankie's hanging precariously from his shirtsleeve and Ms Xavier is clinging to the hair on the back of the Bugman's wrist.

The Bugman notices the spider. He turns. "Nice spider," he says.

While he's distracted, you encourage the butterfly to swoop under his hand and Ms Xavier jumps onto the butterfly's back.

Frankie's hanging on to his sleeve with one hand now, her face red. You're not sure if she can hold on much longer.

"Don't worry, I've got it," Ms Xavier yells. She takes the string and starts tying the end of the rope into a loop.

"Now where's that spray?" the Bugman's voice booms, while you're wheeling the butterfly around face him. Carelessly, he brushes at the butterfly, scattering wing scales.

The poor butterfly is harder to control than ever, but somehow you convince it to swoop down again.

Frankie screaMs

She's going to fall – she's falling! Ms Xavier throws the lasso, catching her around the waist. Together, you pull her up, but before you can get her onto the butterfly's back, Frankie screams and points.

The butterfly's heading straight for the spider's jaws – with you on board. Its fangs are dripping.

You leave Ms Xavier to drag Frankie to safety, and navigate the butterfly, up, up, and away from danger.

Below you, the enormous spider opens its jaws. It's going to eat the Bugman!

Maybe not. The Bugman sprays something into its mouth. It smells pepperminty. Peppermint? What is his evil plan now?

The spider hesitates.

"Oh no, that was my breath-mint spray." The Bugman holds up a hand. "Wait a minute—"

The spider doesn't wait, it pounces, sinking its fangs into the Bugman's arm.

The Bugman howls in pain and drops the remote.

You fly the butterfly over to the discarded transmogrifier – you're probably safe enough while the spider is busy wrapping the Bugman in masses of silk.

You all jump down and rush for the remote. "I guess this is an emergency," Frankie says. She stomps as hard as she can on the black button.

The world spins. Suddenly, everything doesn't feel quite so huge. Even the spider is no longer huge – wait, the spider's gone and a mouse (smelling of peppermint) runs away.

"Blistering beetles, let me go!" the Bugman's muffled voice can just be heard through his thick cocoon of spider silk.

"I think we'll just wait a moment," says Ms Xavier. "Besides, the paramedics should see you before you move."

The paramedics come and go, bundling the Bugman, cocoon and all, onto a stretcher.

Ms Xavier turns to you and Frankie. "Now, I've seen what you can two can do, I think I can safely offer you a position in the prestigious WOS, you know, the World of Spies."

"Ah," Frankie says. "My answer's the same as always. It's no."

"Frankie, you don't have a choice," Ms Xavier says. "Besides, we have an excellent engineering program with access to the best laboratories in the world. And you'll have a special dispensation to work on anything, absolutely anything you want to. The only rule is you have to tell us before you try out any new invention."

"That's okay, I guess," Frankie grumbles. "But what's the other choice?"

"Do I really need to tell you?" Ms Xavier says sternly.

"I guess not," Frankie says. "But how about my new friend?" She looks over at you.

"Ah, for you," Ms Xavier smiles. "I think you could be a pilot in our new experimental aircraft division. It's great pay, the best, even while you're training. Even while you're still at school. How about you give it a go?"

You agree, because going back to your ordinary life would be dull after today. But before you can ask any questions, half Ms Xavier's class gathers around. Kennedy smiles at you and says, "Someone's about to have a lot of detentions."

They all cheer. Which is weird. But what better way to hide a secret training scheme?

"Shush, that's enough," Ms Xavier says. "I think it's time everyone went home." When everyone else has gone home, you and the rest of Ms Xavier's WOS kids are brought to the WOS headquarters. Frankie insists you have a party.

Everyone's dancing and eating pizza and lemonade. Somehow, by the end of the night there have been over twenty speeches and you've been given a strange piece of paper. What the heck, you think, and draw a smiley face on it.

It takes some work, but you become master flyer, taking on several new experimental aircraft as well as a dragon named Cupcake. After discovering Cupcake, you never fly another machine, after all, no aircraft could ever be better than a monstrous lizard that can breathe fire on your enemies from above. Cupcake is brilliant, and will do almost anything for a wheel of specialty cheese

After you retire, you, Cupcake, and the rest of your

family move out to a farm in the middle of Nowhere. It's the most secret farm district in the country, and the best place to raise a young family of dragonlings. (Although they do scare off the unicorns)

It's a long and eventful life, but at the end, you look back and wonder how different your adventures might have been if you had made different life choices. Yes, being eaten alive is a risk, but how bad can it be? Besides there's always the chance you'll become a cheesemaker, how awesome is that? Maybe you could secretly diversify and make specialty cheeses for dragons.

For more adventure, click on a link to:

Go back to *Jeremy Wilder at the Museum.* P10

Or

Go to the Adventure Contents and choose any path. P184

Attack the Ant with the Mini Screwdriver

Holding the mini screwdriver like a sword, you stride toward the ant and clobber it on its head.

"Watch out, behind you!" Frankie yells.

It's another ant. You turn to face its spiky jaws. Its feelers writhe toward you.

You lift the screwdriver to attack.

Thud.

The blow you gave the ant reverberates up your arm, but the ant keeps coming.

You raise the screwdriver to attack again.

The first ant rushes to flank you. It crunches into your arm, snapping the bone, like it's a twig.

You howl in pain, dropping the screwdriver.

More ants are coming.

You run.

Frankie drops the sugar packet and runs, too. But that only attracts more ants. Soon they overwhelm you, their jaws tearing the flesh from your bones. As your consciousness leaves your body, you look down to see nothing more than a skeleton, picked clean.

I'm sorry, you've been eaten. The world of bugs is a dangerous one. Next time you head out on adventure, you may fly a dragon, or be turned into a mouse. You never know what fun awaits while you're busy trying to save the world.

For more adventure, click on a link to:

Go back to *Jeremy Wilder at the Museum.* P10
Or
Go to the Adventure Contents and chose any path. P184

Continue Through to the Rest of the Exhibit

"Bugs, bugs and more bugs," Mr Adams says gleefully as he wanders past all the signs and models. "And look at all the lovely spiders. Aren't they pretty?"

Most of the class don't even bother to look, but a girl with a pink streak through her hair, and a pink shoulder bag decorated with spider webs, rushes past you.

She stares at the Mexican red-kneed tarantula.

The spider's trying to hide under a rock, but it's squished against the glass. If you look closely, you can see its fangs.

"So pretty," she murmurs.

"Course, you'd think so, Spider Girl," someone from Ms Xavier's class says, and high fives their mates.

The girl grins. "Spider Girl. Awesome. That makes me a super hero."

She's grinning, so maybe she won't mind if you do call her Spider Girl.

A boy in a bug t-shirt turns and points. "Oh look, there's a butterfly enclosure. Aren't they gorgeous?"

"Come on, everyone," Mr Adams says. "Team up

with the person next to you. And start filling out these worksheets." He holds out a sheaf of papers. "I've got some spares here if anyone needs one."

Everyone's paired up with their friends, except the girl with the pink streak and the boy in the bug t-shirt who's gone from staring at the butterfly exhibit to sketching a weta in his notebook. He's paying careful attention to get the spikes just right.

You need to make a decision, do you team up with:

Spider Girl? P126
Or
The boy drawing the weta? P141

Team Up with Spider Girl

You hurry toward the girl with the pink streak.

She smiles at you. "Hi, I'm Rose. Have you got your worksheet?" Before you can say anything, she rifles through her pink shoulder bag. "Don't worry, I've got an extra one. "Ah, here it is."

The sheet falls out of a notebook covered with super heroines. Mostly they're hanging from spider webs.

"How about we do spiders?" she says. "Do you see this little tarantula here? She's a girl. I can tell because she doesn't have special hairs called fusillae."

"Okay." She really is a total spider nerd. Which is great because she's busy doing all the work and talking a mile a minute as she fills in the form. She's not even looking at the info board as she runs from one spider exhibit to the next, pointing out the different spiders. The prettiest one is the coastal peacock spider (Maratus speciosus) from Western Australia. It's a tiny little thing with a bright blue metallic abdomen, cute orange markings, and white hairs on its face and legs. It looks a bit like it's been snowed on.

A video of it doing its little dance is playing on a screen.

Rose, the Spider Girl, says, "You should see the video of *Maratus speciosus* playing the bongos on the internet, it's so cute. Just not as cute as Robin Hood, my pet Brown Huntsman. She used to jump on people's heads and freak them out all the time until my Grandma squished her."

Someone in a green mask enters the room. "Mwah ha ha ha," he yells. "I am the Bugma—"

He's cut off by someone at the back of the room. "You work here. You're wearing a museum shirt!" they yell.

The guy's pretty skinny, like the tour guide who stole Frankie's transmogrification remote. Then you notice the guy's still wearing his nametag. Jeremy Wilder. He is the tour guide.

The Bugman (aka Jeremy Wilder) glares in frustration before continuing, "As I was saying, I am the Bugman, soon to be Grand Ruler and Greatest Entomologist of the Whole World. Prepare to bow to my will."

"You can't possibly be the greatest entomologist in the world," says Rose. "I am."

"Ahem," says the boy who was rushing after the butterflies. "I'm the greatest entomologist. You're just the greatest arachnologist."

"Whatever, butterfly boy."

Half the class cracks up laughing.

Ms Xavier isn't taking it so lightly. She rushes out in front of everyone. "Please stay away from my students. They're busy working."

"Pay attention, I'm not fooling around." The Bugman points Frankie's transmogrifier at Ms Xavier.

She shrinks before your eyes. Soon she's no bigger than a bug on the floor.

"Toxic tarantulas," Rosie curses. "That contraption of Frankie's really did work." The class is no longer having fun. No one is laughing, and all chatter has stopped

You look at Rose. "We can't leave Ms Xavier like this. If you distract him, I'll figure out something."

Nodding, she approaches Jeremey Wilder. "Mr Bug man," she says, "I love spiders, please don't hurt them."

"I'd never hurt spiders." Mr Bugman laughs a reedy laugh. "In fact, I'm going to use them to take over the world."

He's definitely distracted now. There are three things you could do:

Grab the remote? P129

Or

Rush to save Ms Xavier? P134

Or

Help Rose distract the Bugman? P136

Grab the Remote

Bravely, you sneak up and snatch the remote from the Bugman's hands – just as he fires it.

There's a flash of light. In seconds, you're as tiny as the Bugman's thumbnail.

Above you, people are screaming and rushing around. You run, ducking left and right to avoid being trampled.

Your hand hurts – it's holding on very tightly to Frankie's transmogrifier. If only you knew how it worked, or had time to look. There must be somewhere safe. You dodge another foot. There's a table! You run toward it.

"Hooray!" one of the giant students yells in a deep booming voice. From your perspective, it's hard to see what's happening, but it looks like they've restrained the Bugman. At least you hope they have. There's a huge leering grasshopper mask not so far away. You glance over again, but you can't see a thing, there's too many feet in the way.

A tiny person rushes up to you. Ms Xavier. Of course.

"Run!" you yell as a black shoe the size of a house looms overhead.

You both run as fast as you can.

"Head for the table," you yell. "If we can shelter under it, we'll be okay. It's not far now."

Something large and brown is scuttling under the table. A cockroach!

"Oh no! Cockroaches!" Ms Xavier says. "I hate cockroaches." She pulls off one of her sensible shoes and starts swatting at the creature.

Another cockroach appears.

"We have to get out of here." You point Frankie's remote at the attacking cockroach. There's a blue button, a pink button and a black button. You randomly push the blue button. Hey, better to test it on bugs than people.

Whoosh. The cockroach grows fast, upsetting the table as it heads to attack the rest of the class.

Over the screams and crashing furniture, Ms Xavier yells, "Quick, press the other button." She's given up on her shoe and is hitting a cockroach over the head with her handbag. It doesn't seem to be doing much damage either. Which is a problem, because another six are on the way.

Pink button or black button? All at once, you realise you could turn yourself and Ms Xavier big again. Then worry about the cockroaches.

You point the transmogrifier at Ms Xavier and press the blue button.

She starts to grow.

Then you turn the remote on yourself and you're big too – but there's still a giant cockroach terrorizing the rest of the students. Mr Adams is backed into a corner waving

the worksheets ineffectually at the creature - like a heavily armored giant insect could be beaten back by homework!

You look at the remote. Pink or black? Which one will shrink the monstrous cockroach before it does more damage? Although, to be fair, it is eating Mr Adam's worksheets, so it's not all bad.

Rose calls, "Press pink, it's my lucky colour."

So you do.

The giant cockroach shrinks. It's still chewing on the worksheets, so they shrink too.

Mr Adams wipes chewed bits of paper from his trousers. "Don't worry, I can always print out more."

Everyone groans, except Rose and the butterfly boy. They both turn in their completed worksheets.

"You put my name on that too, didn't you?" you whisper to Rose.

"Course," Rose says. She bends down and scoops up the cockroach. "I'm going to call you Howie, the homework eater."

Congratulations, you've made a new friend and saved Mr Adams, and perhaps even the whole world. Who knows how much trouble the Bugman would have been if he'd kept Frankie's remote.

The following day, Ms Xavier moves you and Kennedy into her class. She's also let Rose bring Howie the Homework Eater to school, which seems weird, but Ms

Xavier says it's important to face their fears and not blow little things like a small outbreak of giant insects out of proportion. So, he's now officially the class mascot.

You get a week's worth of detentions for no reason. It's totally horrifying, until you realise you're really working with a secret team of trainee spies. As soon as you've figured it out, Ms Xavier gives you the title of Spy in Training, and then it's detention every day for the rest of your school life. Or survival club – depending on who you're talking to. Basic spy training starts with Lying 101. To be fair, the lessons are all about survival skills.

On your last day of school ever, you're finally brought to the WOS (World of Spies) headquarters with Rose and find out you're both already famous for saving Ms Xavier. You climb the stairs to the stage, where she gives you, and several other recruits a piece of paper.

After all your spy training, you're pretty sure it's not blank, but it takes a lot of testing before you realise that to read it you have to wave a black light over it during a full moon. "Congratulations for becoming a member of our prestigious organization," it says. There's even a picture of a button, with a small caption underneath. Press this button and you can join the WOS mailing list. You never know when or where you might find an adventure, in fabulous locations, like on the train, the bus, airplanes and

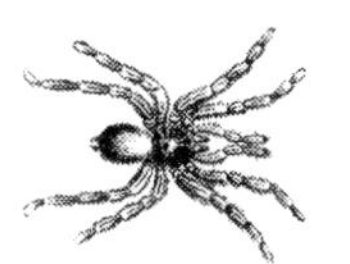

even your own bedroom. Also, watch out for underground bunkers and discounts on books.

Now you've completed your mission and become a spy, you're able to go back into the past using Frankie's new patented Wonder Time Link Technology. Do you want to know what would have happened if you'd made different decisions in the museum that day? Maybe you could have discovered a self-destructing lair, how to solve spy codes, or a kid in a onesie looking for a balloon.

The machine is right in front of you, and on the screen it says, *For more adventure, click on a link to*:

Go back to *Jeremy Wilder at the Museum*. P10

Or

Go to the Adventure Contents and choose any path. P184

Rush to Save Ms Xavier

As you bend to pick up Ms Xavier, the Bugman turns Frankie's device on you. There's a flash of light. Suddenly you're as small as a thumbnail.

Ms Xavier frowns at you. "That's the worst rescue attempt I've ever seen, but at least you tried."

"Thanks," you say.

A shadow looms over your heads. The Bugman's foot, and it's coming down fast.

You run, but not fast enough. The last thing you see is Ms Xavier rolling away. She's escaped, but you're going to be squished and eaten by insects!

Which would have been the end of this adventure – but something weird happens. Time unwinds.

(Later you find out that after Ms Xavier returns to her normal size, she gets Frankie to create a time machine, just to rescue you.)

The foot raises, and hovers above you, like it's stuck in suspended animation. It's Frankie. She's holding a strange notebook. "Quick, we only have a moment."

She shoves the weird notebook in front of your face. "You need to make a different decision, or all you'll get is a posthumous medal for bravery. It's kind of pretty, but is it really worth it? To avoid death, choose one of these three options:"

Help Rose distract the Bugman. P136

Or

Grab the remote. P129

Or

Go to the Adventure Contents and choose any path. P184.

Help Rose Distract the Bugman

While you and Rose are talking to the Bugman, Mr Adams gets braver. He emerges from behind a giant model of a termite mound and helps evacuate the class and the miniature Ms Xavier.

When the conversation slows, you mention the pretty spider with its woggly spider dance.

The Bugman looks amused. Rose says, "Yes peacock spiders are awesome. But I prefer tarantulas." Within minutes they're arguing so loudly neither of them notice the swat team in camouflage gear creeping up on them. Heart in mouth, you wonder if you should move, or talk, or do something to help. Then one of the swat team's boots squeak.

The Bugman raises his remote. "Traitors! You have betrayed me!"

You dive out of the way, pulling Rose to safety. The beam of light grazes her bag, you expect it to shrink like Ms Xavier, but nothing happens, unless you count a grey-black singe on the side.

"Phew, that was close," Rose says.

The guy with the squeaky boots tackles the Bugman, knocking Frankie's remote from his hand.

Before you can catch it, the remote hits the floor, and smashes into a pile of plastic and circuit boards.

The Bugman is on the floor with two of the swat team standing over him when Frankie arrives. "Oh, no," she says, and starts to cry. "I'd recognise those circuit boards anywhere. That took me a month to make. How could you?"

The swat team looks over at her nervously. "That's Frankie, isn't it? She's not going to attack us with monsters or anything, is she?" a burly guy mutters. "I've heard the stories."

Their commander shrugs. "Buck up. We've got a job to do."

"Wait a minute," Rose says. "Where's Ms Xavier?"

"Oh, I've got her," Mr Adams holds up his hand.

Ms Xavier is sitting on it eating a jellybean as big as her head.

"Oh, dear," Frankie says.

"What do you mean, oh dear?" Ms Xavier squeaks. "I am going to turn back to normal size, aren't I?"

"Um—"

The tiny Ms Xavier glares at Frankie.

Frankie gathers up her pile of circuit boards and plastic. "I'll see what I can do."

The next day at school, you're told you've been moved to Ms Xavier's class. You hurry in late. Ms Xavier's voice is booming out over a loudspeaker. "Hurry up and sit down!"

You look around, but still can't see her.

Catching sight of you, Rose waves. Frankie's there too, snoring gently. You go over and sit in the empty desk next to them.

"Shush," says Rose. "She's been up all night trying to fix her contraption. Pleased to see you're now a spy with us."

"A what?"

"Oh, haven't they told you yet? Don't worry, you can be an entomologist with me. It's safer than being a spy. Well, usually."

Spy?

There's a squeak of feedback from the loudspeaker. "Hush," Ms Xavier says.

Everyone covers their ears, groaning from the awful noise.

Finally you see Ms Xavier. She's hopping over to the overhead projector on a bridge made out of rulers and science laboratory retort clamps. "Well," she says to the class, "I'd like to congratulate two people. The budding arachnologists in our class, and the only people, besides Eric, to turn in their homework. Without them, the whole city, maybe even the whole world, would be a very different place right now."

It's probably not a good time to mention that Rose did the worksheet, so you just nod and try not to make a fuss. Two new classes in less than a week. That has to be a record. You don't want a third.

Later, when your spy training is almost complete, you're brought to the WOS headquarters where they shower you with praise and give you a blank certificate.

Frankie looks at it. "I bet that's my patented paper. How dare they? Anyway, it's not that good. It only ever works under a full moon, and that's providing you have a black light to wave over it. Terrible stuff."

From a doll sized podium, with giant WOS flags as a backdrop, the still-tiny Ms Xavier gives a big long boring speech about duty, and saving the world. But it doesn't matter - you, Rose, and Frankie have already decided that the WOS (World of Spies) world isn't for you.

Rose wants to be an entomologist, and Frankie is determined to be an inventor – although she's given up on returning Ms Xavier to her normal size, especially as Ms Xavier insists she'd rather be small. "It's amazing how useful my size is," she says. "I can get anywhere without anyone noticing. Not to mention, the food's better, and I'm really saving on living costs."

Eventually you tell Ms Xavier that you're not going to become a spy, because you're going to do a double degree in biology and engineering. That way you can work with your friends to make tiny bug-sized robots. From time to time, the WOS and other important organizations call on your expertise.

Sometimes you wonder what would have happened if you'd made different decisions. Would you have enjoyed being a spy after all? Learning how to crack codes and use exploding gum might be fun. Or would you rather join the Bugman, and find out what life would be like as an evil minion?

For more adventure, click on a link to:

Go back to *Jeremy Wilder at the Museum*. P10
Or
Go to the Adventure Contents and choose any path. P184

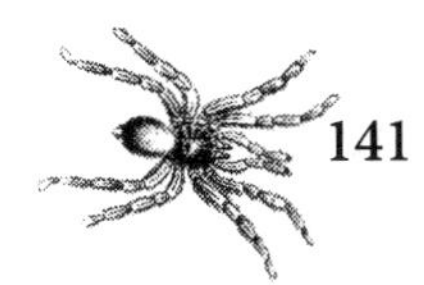

Team Up with the Boy Drawing the Weta

You wander over to the boy in the bug shirt.

He keeps on drawing the weta.

You tap him on the shoulder, and he glances up suspiciously.

"Um, hi," you say.

"Oh, right, you're the new kid. I'm Eric Williams," he says, talking really fast. "Don't worry about the project. I've already done it. So, what do you think of this?" He holds up a completed worksheet. "Didn't want to waste my time filling it in when I could be looking at all the insects."

He shows you his sketches: butterflies, weta, bumble bees, and something called an antlion. They're pretty cool. "Come on," he says, all excited. "Let's look at the ants. Aren't they amazing? They can carry up to fifty times their own weight." He starts sketching again.

A door bangs. You turn. Someone in an ugly grasshopper mask peers in, through a staff only door, before walking through.

"Hey, who's that?" you ask. Then you see his museum shirt. The name tag's still on it: Jeremy Wilder. The tour guide? He's skinny enough, so it must be.

Eric, the bug boy, points at Jeremy Wilder as he wanders past the fire alarm. "Leaping Locusts. Why would the tour guide dress up in an inaccurate bug mask?" Eric says. "It's not even Halloween."

Jeremy Wilder hurries toward you, yelling, "Mwah ha ha ha, I am the Bugman, soon to be Grand Ruler and Greatest Entomologist in all the world. Prepare to bow to my will."

Do you:

Ask Jeremy Wilder, "Why?" **P143**

Or

Stay silent and see what happens? **P153**

Ask Jeremy Wilder, "Why?"

"How dare you question me?!" Jeremy Wilder points a remote at you – no, it's not a remote, it's Frankie's transmogrifier.

A light shines on both you and Eric, The world appears to spin and grow, and in seconds you're the size of insects.

"Cool!" says Eric. "I've always wondered what it would be like to be small." He drags you out of the way of giant footsteps that are running up to confront the Bugman.

Ms Xavier? She's so big it's hard to tell. But they definitely look like her sensible shoes.

A voice rings out. "Jeremy Wilder. What are you up to this time?" You're sure it's Ms Xavier's, but it seems much deeper than usual, and very loud.

"I'm going to take over the world and become an all-powerful overlord. Bow to my rule." His voice booms too.

"Hey!" You turn to Eric. "We have to stop him. There has to be something we can do." You spot the fire alarm. If only you could reach it.

"Insects can do lots of things," Eric says. "Size isn't everything." He pulls out his phone to call someone, but it doesn't work. "At least I can take a selfie," he says.

He gets you both in the viewer, pulls a face and takes a shot.

"But why doesn't your phone work properly?" you ask. "There must be a reason."

"Physics is different at this size."

"So we could climb walls?"

"Yeah, why not? Most insects can."

The fire alarm appears to be very far away, but you have to try. "See the fire alarm? If we can make it, we might be able to stop him."

Despite your size, you can move pretty quickly, bounding bigger distances than you thought you'd be able to. Getting up the wall is pretty easy, so long as you don't look down. Getting past the glass is slightly more difficult. Together, you and Eric lever it out as far as you can before slipping in behind it and jumping up and down on the switch.

The class is already heading out the door, burdened by huge terrariuMs "Quick," you yell. "We need to jump as hard as we can. One, two, three – jump."

Eric slips, as the switch flicks on, and the alarm begins to ring.

You grab his arm, "Hold on tight." The noise is unbelievably loud, and it's hard to hold on with Eric scrabbling to regain his footing.

He slips again. You clench your teeth and haul him up.

The Bugman stops in his tracks. "Who did that!?" He runs around pointing the transmogrification remote at students – shrinking nine people before he stops and orders everyone who is left to pick up the terrariums again.

On the ground, six of the miniature students are having a selfie party, determined to photograph themselves next to everything. The favorite item is a paperclip. They lean on it, hold it up in the air, and wear it like a giant hat.

Eric nudges you. "Look."

Three students and Ms Xavier are under a table, fighting off two giant cockroaches.

"Quick," you say, thinking fast, and talking between siren blares as you climb down the wall. "We need to grab that paperclip and rescue them."

"Hey, we need this," you tell the students playing with the paperclip. Together, you and Eric make it into a long pointy thing – a cross between a sword and a twisted spear and run over to Ms Xavier and the students fighting off the cockroaches.

By the time you get to them, Ms Xavier is looking ragged. She has bites out of her clothing and she's missing her purse and one of her shoes.

Leaping in, fearlessly, you stab one of the cockroaches.

It scuttles away.

The fire alarm stops, but other sirens can be heard in the distance, even over the Bugman screaming that there aren't enough people to carry the terrariums.

A SWAT team sneaks in. They're as loud as a herd of elephants, their footsteps shaking the ground. The giant letters on the flak jackets say "WOS – World of Security."

The second cockroach lunges at you. Bravely, you raise the paperclip, but this time the cockroach doesn't back off. It snaps at the sliver of steel, grabbing it and throwing it aside. Its enormous mouth is coming right at you.

You're going to be eaten! It's biting your arm!

Eric shoulder barges into the armored brute, and you wrench free.

A light shines from above.

Suddenly, you're proper sized again. Eric, Ms Xavier, and some of the other kids are too.

Ms Xavier squashes the cockroach with her remaining shoe. "Horrible creatures," she says.

Eric shrugs. "They're not so bad when they're not trying to eat you."

"I'll take your word for it," Ms Xavier says. "Has everyone been rescued yet?" She begins to counts all the students, then searches the floor. A girl with a pink spider bag appears.

Looking sheepish, Kennedy, Steve and a few others return with Frankie in tow. Frankie brushes cobwebs from

her clothing. Some of the students with her also look worse for wear. Their clothes are splattered with blue, like they're three years old and painting the sky in art class. Or as if they'd re-enacted a horror movie with blue blood.

After the last student has been found, Mr Adams reappears with coffee in hand. "Goodness, whatever happened?" he says. "Lucky you were here to sort it out, hey Ms X?"

Ms Xavier glares at him, but says nothing.

"I wouldn't like to be him," Eric says. "I've heard Ms Xavier holds a grudge."

She seems to like you, though. She congratulates you and Eric for your bravery and offers you both a job at some kind of secret organization called WOS – either in the science department or as a spy. Eric shakes his head. "No, I don't want anything to do with WOS, both my parents are agents and they're the most boring people I know. I'm going to be an entomologist. I believe bugs will save the world. The Bugman just had it a little bit wrong. We should use co-operation, not force, and work together.

You have a choice. Do you:

Become an entomologist? P151

Or

Join WOS (World of Spies) as a spy? P148

Join WOS as a Spy

You take Eric's place in Ms Xavier's class. At first, it's pretty quiet except Ms Xavier gives you a ton of detentions.

Then you notice that the worksheets you have to do in detention all have encoded puzzles down the bottom. The rest is all fluff for the naughty kids.

You're being taught half a dozen codes, including simple replacement codes

The first replacement code you learn replaces letters with numbers. The key is: A=1, B=2 all the way to Z=26 Can you solve the message below?

§

23-5-12-12 4-15-14-5

§

The Caesar Shift Cipher is another handy code for any aspiring spy. Here, Ms Xavier moved the cipher six to the left so A=V and B=W etc. (You could also choose to read it the other way around with A=F, but Ms X doesn't like it that way, and it won't work for the example.)

Xjibmvopgvodjin!

One of the last (so called) *simple replacement codes* you learn is the atbash cipher. Atbash is another form of replacement cipher, but uses the alphabet backwards to encrypt messages. So A in a message becomes Z, B becomes Y etc. See if you can decipher the following message – it's pretty tricky.

§

Vcxvoovmg, blf'iv z nzhgvi xlwv yivzpvi!

§

Now you've figured out how to solve codes, you're well on the way to becoming a spy. The World of Spies holds a special ceremony to make you one of their own. It's a massive party with cake and pizza and ice-cream and you get a very special spy ID. It looks just like an ordinary school ID unless you look at it beneath a WOS torch on the Doppler setting. You also get your very own WOS torch, a laser pen and ten different types of gum, from explosive to edible, including your favorite, Forget-Me Gum.

During the ceremony, Ms Xavier congratulates you for rescuing her from the cockroaches. It seems no one even realises that you and Eric saved the world from the Bugman by setting off the fire alarm. But you don't mind, because now that you're a real spy you can join the WOS mailing list by pressing this button. You can check out the books anywhere, in all kinds of fabulous locations, like on the train, the bus, airplanes and even your own bedroom.

Sometimes you wonder what would have happened if you'd chosen another path. You chat with Frankie, and she says, "Let's find out." She offers you her time machine. ***You have five choices:***

1. Help Frankie

Or

2. Help Kennedy

Or

3. Join Eric as an Entomologist

Or

4. Go back to *Jeremy Wilder at the Museum*. P10

Or

5. Go to the Adventure Contents and choose any path. P184

Become an Entomologist

The life of an entomologist is full of excitement and adventure. When you're not in the lab, you get to fly all over the world and hunt for new species of bugs. You name three of them after your friends, Frankie, Kennedy and Eric.

Sometimes Eric and you team up on really big projects, like making the biggest buggiest adventure park in the world. But the best fun of all, is going to schools and telling people all about the exhilarating and dangerous world of bugs.

From time to time, the World of Spies and other important organizations call on your expertise, but you don't always give it. They just don't understand the importance and wonder of bugs. Too often, you find yourself explaining that without bugs, the world would fall apart, and we'd all starve to death.

People from all around the world congratulate you on your amazing work. But sometimes you wonder what would it would be like to take a different path. Would you be eaten by spiders, dragged into an antlion pit trap, or live to save the day?

When you're ready, you may want to try another adventure, braving untold horrors so that you can live a wonderful life as a spy and retire on a desert island with a two hundred year supply of marmalade, live on a desolate farm in a place called Nowhere, or visit Martians.

For more adventure click on a link to:

Go back to *Jeremy Wilder at the Museum*. P10

Or

Go to the Adventure Contents and Choose any path. P184

Stay Silent and See What Happens

Ms Xavier steps forward and yells at the Bugman, "Stop. Back away from my students." She's standing in front of the class protecting everyone. What's she doing there all by herself? You look around for Mr Adams but he's nowhere to be seen. Kennedy's also disappeared, and Frankie's long gone.

This is turning out to be a strange field trip, but how much trouble can a man in a lousy grasshopper mask be?

He pulls something from his pocket. It's Frankie's transmogrifier. It can't work, surely?

The Bugman aims it at Ms Xavier. A beam of light shines on her and she shrinks, until you only think you can see her on the floor. A little smaller than a thumb, she's hard to see with her green and brown clothing.

Some of the students scream, but you surprise yourself by bravely taking a step closer. Maybe you can rescue Ms Xavier?

"Ignore that," the Bugman says, waving the remote in the direction of the class. "Pick up these terrariums and follow me, or you'll be next."

Eric nudges you with his elbow and reaches down to pick up the tiny, Ms Xavier.

"Stop that," the Bugman screams at him. "I warned you. Help with the terrariums or I'll shrink both you and your friend."

Eric coughs. "Um, I was just trying to find my contact lens. I've dropped it here somewhere."

Do you:

Help Eric look for Ms Xavier? P155

Or

Obey instructions and grab a terrarium? P166

Help Eric Look for Ms Xavier

"Hey, Mr Bugman," you say. "Eric can't see without his contact lenses. It'll be quicker if I help look."

The Bugman sighs and points Frankie's transmogrifier at a couple of ants he's pulled out of a terrarium. The ants grow until they're the size of bulldogs.

"I don't have time for your nonsense," the Bugman says, spraying the giant ants with a can labelled Bugman Patented Ant Spray. "Now, get to work," the Bugman snaps. "And ants, you can eat the stragglers."

Eric puts Ms Xavier on his shoulder, and nudges you, pointing to where she's sitting. She's rifling through her handbag as if nothing is wrong.

You glance nervously at the Bugman. "Awesome, Eric, you found your lenses. How about giving me a hand?" After all, there's no point in rescuing Ms Xavier, if you're both going to be eaten by ants.

Eric winks and helps you grab a terrarium as five ants escort everyone out an emergency exit, after the Bugman.

Outside is a small courtyard, surrounded by statues. The Bugman has rushed over to an elephant statue and is sitting next to its feet. You can't really see much, there are too many people in the way, and you're carrying a very large terrarium.

"Quick, quick!" the Bugman shouts, standing up and waving the transmogrifier. People start disappearing down an open hatch underneath the elephant. You follow them down a short flight of stairs to a long dark passageway.

Lights from several rooms sneak out from under the doors. Then the lights flick on.

"There, that's better," the Bugman says. "Now hurry up, let's get moving."

A door opens. As you pass by you peer in. There are about fifty people sitting at computers and wearing t-shirts with WOE on the back and World Wide Web of Envelopes on the front.

"Hey," Eric whispers. "Ms Xavier says to drop her off in this room near a computer." He slows to talk to a red-headed boy in ratty jeans behind you. "Here Joe, help my friend with this. Careful, don't let the Bugman see." The red-headed boy winks and grabs the terrarium.

Eric disappears into the computer room.

Just a few yards down the corridor, the Bugman stops. He looks at the ants waving their feelers wildly, and then up and down the corridors. It seems very much like the ants are communicating with him. He counts everyone.

"Who's missing? Where is that aggravating boy with the bug t-shirt?"

Someone at the front yells, "He must have gone to the bathroom, sir."

There's a flash.

The Bugman's turns the shrink ray on whoever it was.

The class gasps and shuffles back. Another person has been shrunk! You need to make a decision—

Do you:

Tell the Bugman where Eric went? P158

Or

Keep quiet and hope Eric and Ms Xavier are okay? P162

Tell the Bugman Where Eric Went

"Sir," you say. "Please don't shrink any more people. Eric just went through that door."

"Traitor!" Joe yells. He drops the terrarium, sending insects and shards of glass flying.

"Ow!" there's a large spike of glass in your leg. Maybe not that large, but it hurts a lot. Carefully, you pull it out.

The Bugman laughs. "Come on then. Let's go find him." He leads the way back to the computer room. At first you don't see Eric because he's wearing a World of Envelopes t-shirt and is hiding behind a desk.

"Ah, there you are!" The Bugman shouts. He's spotted Eric. You can tell, because he's pointing the transmogrifier right at him. Then he smiles and shrinks Eric.

"Oh my goodness, and what do we have here," the Bugman says, grabbing at something hiding behind the computer mouse.

It's Ms Xavier.

"Mwah ha ha ha," the Bugman squashes Ms Xavier under his hand. "How dare you defy me!" he yells. "I am

the Bugman, the most dangerous supervillain you have ever seen—I mean, you will ever see." He holds out the transmogrifier. "Wait a minute, what was I doing? Here have a t-shirt."

He pulls a t-shirt from a shelf. "This looks about your size. I got them made especially, but these idiots wouldn't wear them." He glares around the room.

They all hurry to put on the new shirts, which still have WOE on the back, but instead of World of Envelopes emblazoned on the front, World of Entomology is stitched over the silhouettes of various insects. After you put it on, the Bugman claps his hand around your shoulders. "I like you," he says. "And my ants do too. I think I have the perfect job for you. One moment." He sprays something at two of the ants and they scurry off.

"Now, follow me, everybody. We're about to change the world." The Bugman marches everyone into a room filled with lab benches. He presses a button and strange funnels drop down from the ceiling like oxygen masks. "Put one funnel into each terrarium, now!" he yells. "And do match the insects with the name on the funnels." He takes his time checking each funnel and the plastic piping attaching them to the ceiling. When he's certain each of the terrariums is properly hooked up, whatever that means, the Bugman and his ants force everyone not wearing a WOS t-shirt into a cell. A sign on the outside says, Insect Food.

"Hey," you say.

"Come on," he says. "Forget about them." He points the transmogrifier at you. "Minions, come, we still have work to do if I am to take over the world." He forces you and the other World of Envelopes t-shirt wearers to walk to the next room. It's lined with giant screens and strange machines with hundreds of buttons and switches and is large enough to fit over twenty of you, including ants. My Evil Plan, is written in large friendly letters on the top of a whiteboard covered with Photoshopped images of militarised insects taking over the world.

The Bugman puts Frankie's transmogrification remote into a drawer in the machine and presses a green button that says happily ever after.

How bad can it be? you wonder, as the screens flicker.

In minutes giant bees are swarming over City Hall, giant spiders are dropping from the skies and giant termites are eating a holes out of the local police station. The Bugman cheers, and some of his hench-people cheer too.

The remaining students (who were quick-thinking enough to have put on World of Entomology t-shirts) are horribly silent as they watch the devastation of Greenville, and the rest of the world unfold. The worst bit is when ants take over the White House.

"Look!" says the Bugman. "With bees in city hall and ants in the White House, things might finally get done. Now

henchmen, get to work, and start looking after the next generation of rulers."

You know the world is about to get a whole lot worse, as the Bugman creates a nest of giant spiders and places you in spider-web chains.

Your orders are to look after the baby army ants. So you shuffle off to the newly dug nursery. The baby ants look like white boogers as they sway and wiggle for food and attention. It's a miserable life. Sometimes you dream of what might have been if you hadn't betrayed Eric and Ms Xavier.

Maybe you could have saved the world, and then celebrated with cake and lemonade, or earned the golden key to the WOS zoo, so you could visit any time for free. On the other hand, you could have died horribly and have nothing but a statue to honor your bravery, or a time machine to get you out of trouble. It's hard to know, unless you really could go back into the past. But that's impossible isn't it? Then, one day, you come across a strange piece of weird paper that feels like very fine, soft chainmail.

It says:

Click here to go back to *Jeremy Wilder at the Museum*. P10

Or

Go to the Adventure Contents and pick any part of the adventure. P184

Keep Quiet and Hope Eric and Ms Xavier are Okay

You bravely say nothing, not even flinching when the Bugman threatens you with the transmogrifying remote.

Some of the students are crying as the Bugman shrugs and says, “Pathetic. I was going to let you see me take over the world, but now I have a better idea.”

He takes you through a series of interconnected corridors, and down into a high-ceilinged arena that once must have held a swimming pool. Now the pool is filled with sand.

“Mwah ha ha ha,” the Bugman laughs. “Welcome to the Sand Pit. Home of the soon-to-be-amazing giant antlion. Who’d like to be first up for dinner?”

Everyone steps back.

The Bugman points to someone holding a sand-filled terrarium. “You,” he says. “You two with the antlion terrarium, bring it here and I’ll spare your life.”

“That’s us,” Joe whispers. He shuffles forward.

“Wait,” you whisper.

He doesn't stop. You're very close now, close enough that you could almost reach out and touch Frankie's transmogrifier in his hand.

"Now!" Joe yells and you drop the terrarium on his foot, duck away from his reaching arms, and dive behind a nearby seat.

A loudspeaker squeaks. The feedback is so terrible, you want to cover your ears, but you can't because you're holding a terrarium.

"Stop!" the voice thunders. "Jeremy Wilder. You are surrounded. Drop the weapon, there's no escape."

"Never," the Bugman yells. He grabs you out from behind the seat, and waves the transmogrifier threateningly at your face. "Mwah ha ha ha. You'll never stop me." He waves the transmogrifier around, singeing seats and lighting up patches of sand.

The sand in the sandpit begins to boil. It's not actually boiling, but erupting with enormous insects.

A mottled black creature emerges from the sand revealing long spindly legs on a leaf-shaped body. Very slowly, it reaches out two black claw-like limbs toward the Bugman. You struggle to get away.

Someone yells from behind the highest seats. "Hey, watch out, it's a whip scorpion." It's Butterfly boy, Eric. You can tell by the voice – and the bug t-shirt.

"A whip scorpion?" The Bugman says. You break free as he turns to face the terrifying beast. Frankie's transmogrifier clatters on the tiles at the edge of the pool. The creature grabs him with its claw-like caricature of human hands, pulls him into the pit, and begins to eat – its crunching echoing horribly.

Gunshots ring out. Screams

You duck for cover, and hunker down until the bullets stop. When you look up, the whip scorpion and the Bugman have disappeared into the sand.

Reunited with her transmogrifier, Frankie returns Ms Xavier to her rightful size. Not that it helps Frankie any, she's been given detention for the rest of the year. So have you. You tell anyone who will listen about how unfair it is, but no one listens.

Even Kennedy laughs. "Awesome, you'll love it," she says.

It takes you a week to realise that detention in your new school is really spy training. You become really fit, especially with all the obstacle courses, and really clever with all the extra worksheets. A year later, you're taken to a special ceremony to induct you into World of Spies headquarters. They congratulate you for helping save Ms Xavier, and give you a blank piece of paper. You're not stupid, you know it has code on it, but you hardly care.

What you're most interested in, aside from extra helpings of WOS pizza (it's twice as tasty as real pizza, but three times more dangerous) is an opportunity to visit the President and his or her children when they're elected.

You're going to be vetted so you can become a Junior Secret Service agent and make sure the President's family remains safe, wherever they go.

Well done, you've saved the day, your class, Greenville, and possibly the world. Who knows how much trouble giant bugs could have been? With your new training, you have even more opportunities to do remarkable things. And if saving the world gets boring, you can press this button and join the WOS mailing list. Because even spies like to relax with amazing books.

For more adventure, like feeding ants, fighting a lady bug, or accidentally helping to blow up the museum, click on a link to:

Go back to *Jeremy Wilder at the Museum.* P10

Or

Go to the Adventure Contents and choose any path. P184

Obey Instructions and Grab a Terrarium

You grab a terrarium, and a red-headed boy rushes over to help. "Hi, I'm Joe."

Most of the students hurry to grab terrariums too, as the Bugman shines the transmogrifier onto ants, making them the size of bulldogs, then sprays them with various cans.

"Where's a giant ant-eater when you need one?" Joe, the red-headed boy mutters.

"Shut up," the Bugman says and orders everybody out. "This way — and quick!" He leads you through an emergency exit, out of the museum and into a courtyard filled with statues. With so many people all around, you can't see what's happening. There's a whirring sound and the ants start herding you into an open hatch underneath an elephant statue.

Slowly, you and Joe manhandle the terrarium down the stairs. You're almost there when he trips on the final step.

The terrarium appears to drop in slow motion. You scrabble to get it back under control, swiping at it ineffectually. It smashes. Shards of glass fly everywhere.

The Bugman looks back.

"Was that my whip scorpion?" He looks at the black mottled creature with thin legs and strange limbs with hand-like claws. It's got a shard of glass sticking right through its leaf-shaped body.

"Is it a really a scorpion?" Joe whispers. "It doesn't even have a scorpion tail."

"Fools. Bugs don't need venom to kill you." The Bugman stomps around, looking inside all the terrariuMs He points at one. "Put it down," he says.

He points the transmogrifier at something inside. A praying mantis. It reaches down, picks up Joe and eats him.

Everyone tries to run away.

"Don't drop those terrariums," the Bugman warns as he and the ants usher you all into a room filled with lab benches and strange funnels that drop down from the ceiling like oxygen masks. "See, this," he says. "Isn't it the most beautiful invention you've seen in your life? The tubes will suck up the insects, send them to Frankie's transmogrifier before letting them loose on the world." He holds up his arms as if waiting for applause, but nobody claps or says a word.

"Idiots," the Bugman says, checking the last bit of plastic tubing connecting the funnels to the ceiling. "This way, then." He orders you all in a tiny room and locks the door.

One by one, students are dragged out by giant insects. Some people don't make it out the door before bits of them are bitten off.

There's very few of you left when a praying mantis enters the room. Joe's praying mantis. It grabs you with its big sharp forelegs and bites your head off.

I'm sorry, you've been eaten. The world of bugs is a dangerous one, which is what makes it so exciting. Next time when you head out on adventure, you may like to die a hideous death with new and exciting bugs, save a toddler from an explosion, or have a toddler save you. There's even a chance you'll be taught by a miniature teacher smaller than your thumb.

For more adventure, click on a link to:

Go back to *Jeremy Wilder at the Museum.* P10

Or

Go to the Adventure Contents and choose any path. P184

You Choose: Ant. Grasshopper

On the other side of the rubble, Frankie punches in the two code words while the countdown drones on. "Self-destruct in ten seconds and—"

The countdown stops. Everybody still caught inside cheers.

"Quick!" you say, pulling away rubble to clear a path. Richard and Kennedy lend you a hand. On the inside, Frankie and the other students have formed a human chain, moving rocks away from the slip.

The hole is almost big enough for people to squeeze through when the Bugman arrives with his giant ants. "You meddling kids thwarted my evil plan," he yells. "I will destroy you. Ants, attack!"

His giant ants charge at Frankie and the rest of the survivors. Bravely, they turn to defend themselves.

You scrabble at the hole desperately. People are being eaten. Body parts and blood are scattered amongst the rubble. Finally some of the debris gives way, and you squeeze through with Kennedy and Richard close behind.

"We can't use my exploding gum," Kennedy yells. "It might collapse the whole corridor."

"We'll have to get the transmogrifier off the Bugman," you tell them. Together, you fight your way through the dust and past the ants, picking up bits of rubble and throwing them at the giant insects. Others join in.

The ants have been forced to retreat, but as you approach the Bugman, they rally, their jaws snapping.

You grab a piece of plaster and throw it at the closest ant. It staggers back, but it's not deterred. It picks itself up, jaws wide. Then it bites Kennedy's hand off.

The Bugman's right there waving Frankie's transmogrifier. Richard disappears in a flash of light.

Reaching for another missile, you slip.

The Bugman's noticed. He leaps over.

You roll out of the way.

The ant snaps its jaws, tearing the fabric of your top. You roll back again. The Bugman's pointing Frankie's transmogrifier at you.

There's no one to back you up. It's either die by ant or be transformed by Frankie's machine. In desperation, you grab the Bugman's leg.

He wobbles.

Someone throws plaster at him, and he falls, the remote slipping from his fingers.

You both scrabble for it.

The ant approaches, its jaws wide open. It's going to eat you—

You feel its jaws pierce your arm, and then suddenly it's shrinking.

You must have pressed a button on Frankie's transmogrifier remote. Somehow. Or maybe the Bugman has. Both of you are still wrestling for it, white knuckled and determined not to let it go.

Kennedy, her wrist still bleeding profusely, shoulder-barges the Bugman with her good arm. It's not very hard, she is missing a hand, but it's just enough to help you wrestle Frankie's transmogrifier off the Bugman.

He puts up his hands and surrenders.

Everyone still alive cheers.

You, Kennedy and Richard all receive medals for your bravery. Although Kennedy can't be at the ceremony, she's still too week, and Richard can't be at the ceremony because he's still planning to be a spy. Kennedy's not so sure. "Wait until after I get my robot hand," she says.

The mayor and the town applaud you for your courage.

Ms Xavier brings you back to the World of Spies headquarters, where they also shower you with praise. They give you a blank piece of paper and tell you to wave a black light over it underneath a full moon. The certificate says you're an honorary spy and a partial member of WOS. It's a perfectly useless certificate, you can't even show it to anyone who isn't a World of Spies agent.

The other thing they've given you is much better – it's a mousepad that says, "I saved the world, and all I got was this useless mousepad." Underneath the mousepad is a long button with the words, Need adventure? For help and special offers join the WOS mailing list. Hey why not?

Or you could rewind time and try this adventure again. Frankie says she has a time machine, and Kennedy says her robot hand is cool and all, but it's not the same as having a real one. What would happen if you went back into the past and chose a different path? Would you learn how to solve spy codes, or be attacked by insects that are armored and dangerous? Would you blow up the Bugman's underground lair? Or bring home a pet mouse?

For more adventure, click on a link to:

Go back to *Jeremy Wilder at the Museum*. P10

Or

Go to the Adventure Contents and choose any path. P184

You Choose: Bee. Caterpillar

"Sounds good," Frankie says.

You can hear her typing on the other side of the rubble.

"Self-destruct in ten seconds and count—"

The countdown stops abruptly.

"Hooray," everyone yells. "You've saved the day."

"Anomaly detected," the countdown voice says. "Self-destruct now in five – four – thee – two—"

A rumble. You feel it under your feet. In your teeth. In your eyeballs. Then the whole world explodes, tearing you into tiny fragments of blood and bone and gristle.

Oops. You're very dead. It's probably no consolation to know everybody else is dead and the museum is destroyed, but, if you like, you can take this moment to try one of the other endings. Ant Grasshopper or Cat Lepidoptera.

Or you could go on another adventure; maybe you will fly on the back of a butterfly, save the world with spray cans, or fight off a giant ladybug.

For more adventure, click on a link to:

Go back to *Jeremy Wilder at the Museum*. P10

Or

Go to the Adventure Contents and choose any path. P184

You choose: Cat. Lepidoptera

"Okay," Frankie says. "Here goes."

You can hear beeping from the other side of the rubble. The self-destruct starts talking. "Does not compute, twenty three minutes remaining, and counting."

The others all exchange looks, but there's not much time for anything else before a flash of sound and light hits your senses. When you pick yourself up off the floor, it's hard to stand up.

And then you look down at your paws – PAWS!?!?! You squeak in horror. Somehow, you've been turned into a mouse.

Other mice are turning around and around in circles, squeaking in terror. Although a few are casually washing their whiskers as if nothing is wrong.

"Quick, this way," a mouse says. You're pretty sure it's Frankie. She leads all the other mice through the rubble toward you and then makes a megaphone out of old posters and a bit of wire. It takes a bit of yelling through the megaphone, but the police do eventually come down to see what's happening. Once they see the mouse yelling through the megaphone, they grin. A voice booms out very loudly. "We'd better send for Frankie's mother."

After weeks of living at Frankie's house, drinking terrible potions and getting changed into rubber balls, strawberry plants and jellyfish, you're all turned back into people.

Weeks later, back at home, you receive a mousepad with a cat on it in the mail. On it are the words, I survived The Great Mouse Incident. Never Again. But in the end, it's not so bad, because becoming a mouse made you discover your love of cheese. You move to France and become the best cheesemaker in the world, crafting all kinds of specialty cheeses. Royalty and celebrities are the only people who can afford your most expensive product, Crafty Cupcake's Camembert. Each of these cheeses is worth a time machine. And that's the best part, because you discover there's plenty more adventure to be had by going back in time.

If you make different choices you can blow up the entire museum, join the bad guys, or find your own mouse companion – a diabolical varmint who will plot revenge against you from under the kitchen cupboards.

For more adventure, click on a link to:

Go back to *Jeremy Wilder at the Museum*. P10

Or

Go to the Adventure Contents and choose any path. P184

Insect Glossary

ANT

Ants are a common insect around the world, and some species of ant have been known to lift fifty times their own body weight. More than 12,500 species of ant have been classified. Ants are also related to wasps and bees. Most landmasses on earth have ant species, with a few exceptions such as Antarctica and a few remote inhospitable islands.

ANTLION

The antlion included in this book is a larval antlion, or juvenile – which means it hasn't grown into an adult yet. Juvenile antlions burrow into soft sand or dirt, creating a pit trap. When insects slip inside, the juvenile antlion throws sand at them, forcing them to slip into the pit into the waiting jaws of the antlion.

Due to their lacy wings and stick-like abdomen, adult antlions are commonly mistaken for damselflies. Distinguishing features are their longer clubbed antennae and nocturnal lifestyle.

BUTTERFLY

The Monarch Butterfly is the butterfly species featured in this book. It is commonly found in the Americas, as well as parts of Australia and New Zealand. They are bright orange butterflies with striking black markings. Monarch Butterflies can live to up to eight months in the wild. As caterpillars, they have destinctive black, yellow and white stripes.

BEE

Bees are flying insects that serve an important role in the ecosystem pollinating flowers. The best-known species of bees are the honey bee, for producing honey and beeswax, and the bumblebee, for its large size and fluffy appearance. There are nearly 20,000 recognised species of bees worldwide.

CENTIPEDE

Despite their name, Centipedes have varying numbers of legs depending on the species, and have one pair of legs per body segment. Around 3,000 species of Centipedes have been described. A key trait for centipedes is the venom claw, which helps them catch and kill prey. Centipedes have been around for thousands of years, with fossil records showing they were around before the time of the dinosaurs.

COCKROACH

Over 4,500 species of cockroaches have been discovered, although only thirty species have been known to live alongside humans. Of these, only four are known to be pests. They're very resilient and some have even been known to live without heads.

FLY

There are over 120,000 species of fly known to science, and it is likely that there are many more undiscovered. One of the most common is the housefly. The giant model described in this book is a bluebottle fly. It's called the bluebottle fly, due to the pretty metallic-blue colouring on its body. A common fly species worldwide, it is also often considered a pest.

LADYBIRD

Ladybirds, also known as ladybugs, are not actually true bugs – they are actually beetles. Ladybirds commonly have red, yellow or orange wing covers with black spots. These wing covers are also called wing-cases or carapaces by scientists. These beetles are useful to gardeners because many species eat pests that gardeners consider harmful, like aphids.

PRAYING MANTIS

The Praying Mantis is probably best known because the females cannibalise the males during mating. There are roughly 2,400 species worldwide, commonly found in temperate or tropical habitats. They are typically ground-dwelling ambush predators. Some species of Mantis have become so adapted to hunting around one type of plant, they have evolved a plant-specific camouflage, like the pink Orchid Mantis.

STICK INSECT

Stick insects, also known as walking sticks or stick bugs, are the name for a group of insects which have adapted to look like sticks as a form of camouflage. Against the right background, they can be very hard to see, making them hard for predators to find. Stick Insects are found all over the world, aside from the Antarctic and Patagonia. Which seems very strange, so if they do turn up in Patagonia we will not be surprised.

SPIDER

Spiders have eight legs, and almost all of them have venom and vomit enzymes to help digest their meals. Many spin webs to catch flies and other insects. Two species are featured in this book. Peacock spiders are tiny jumping spiders, growing no more than 0.2 inches in length. They're named for the males' flashy mating display. Male peacock spiders have brightly coloured abdomens with flaps on the sides so their colourful fan can be tucked away when not in use. The tiny, but colourful, peacock spider is found in Australia.

The other group featured spiders are tarantulas. Approximately 900 species of tarantulas have been identified. They are typically large in size and very hairy, which may be why these arachnids have become quite popular in some parts of the world as exotic pets.

SCORPION

Scorpions are arachnids, which means they're related to spiders (and some ticks). They possess eight legs and have two main body parts: a head and an abdomen. But the thing most people notice about a scorpion is its pincers and long tail, tipped with a venomous stinger. These arachnids can be found on all continents except for Antarctica. All scorpions glow under ultra violet light, so if you're out in the dessert at night don't forget to bring a black light to see how many there are.

WETA

These spiny insects are native to New Zealand. There are five main groups: giant weta, cave weta, tree weta, tusked weta and ground weta. They're related to crickets, and range in size from the small cave weta to the giant weta. Unfortunately, many species of weta are threatened by habitat loss and introduced predators.

WHIP SCORPION

The scorpion featured in this book is a tailless whip scorpion, also known as a whip spider. These arachnids are actually a separate species to true whip scorpions. They are pretty harmless to humans as they possess no venomous fangs, and prefer to grab prey with their claws.

Sign Up For New Adventures

THE WOS (World of Spies) MAILING LIST

The World of Spies Newsletter is on the right hand side at the very top of Miss Lionheart's website: misslillylionheart.wordpress.com (https://misslillylionheart.wordpress.com/join-us-at-the-wwwos)

THE WOE (World of Evil) MAILING LIST

The World of Evil Newsletter is right at the top of Lilly's website between *Free Previews* and *Join us at the WWWOS* (https://misslillylionheart.wordpress.com/join-us-at-the-wwwoe)

(The WWWOE and WWWOS marketing people teamed up to cut down on paperwork and improve visibility. But do not fear, this just means that operational secrecy is especially important to us.)

Books

The Frankie Files

Are you ready for **Monsters and Mayhem?**

Frankie wants to be a world-famous inventor, but her inventions always get her into **monster** trouble.

Save the Moa

Gilt Edge

Chris loves looking after the giant weta at Krell Research, but they're old news. The latest project is bringing back the moa, or as Vincent Krell calls it, *de-extinction*. The giant flightless birds are amazing, but they're more dangerous and more trouble than Chris could ever have imagined.

Miss Lionheart's Laboratory of Death

Hijack yourself into mad scientists' territory, duck the gelignite, avoid the Acme fuses. Do whatever you need to, just make sure you don't miss out — it's more than your life is worth.

A mad romp into the dangerous world of evil genius, super spies, and deadly designer animals.

A.J. Ponder

Quest for Merlin

You Choose a Fairytale Adventure

You are Merlin's only hope. *You* choose which path you take, and the stories you discover. Monsters, pirates, mermaids, giants, and more – there's even a fire-breathing, adventurer-eating dragon – and a not-to-be-missed tea party. Each path will test your wits, your bravery, and your strength of heart.

The Great Weta Robbery

When your after-school job is looking after weta the size of cats, it'd be understandable if you thought that your life couldn't get any more exciting or dangerous. But theres a darker secret lurking in the laboratories of Krell Research and it's down to one boy – with his sidekicks Snapper, Fluffy, Five-Legs and the other mega-weta – to get to the bottom of it.

Wizard's Guide to Wellington

"Wizards and a taniwha running wild in Wellington – who would have thought it. Perrin's adventures in the capital city are fun to follow and full of surprises. My (unpointy) hat is off to Alicia Ponder. Now where's my broom..." **Fiona Kidman**

Adventure Contents

Introduction: School Trip 6
Jeremy Wilder at the Museum 10
Stay with the class 12
Sneak through the blue door 14
Rush out through the emergency exit to rescue the class 16
Try and find Ms Xavier 18
Say you have Ms Xavier in your pocket 21
Keep quiet and don't mention Ms Xavier 26
Say you'll join the Bugman 29
Tell the Bugman you'd rather die – *warning, this ending is too scary for one of the authors!* 31
Sneak through the green door 34
Volunteer to help Steve find the Bugman 38
Throw the exploding chewing gum at the ladybug/ladybird 41
Put your hands up and go to stand by the wall with the two scientists 44
Stand up for what you believe in 46
Tell the Bugman you want to join WOE 50
Stay with Steve and defy the Bugman 52
Volunteer to help Kennedy find Ms Xavier and Frankie 55
Race up to fight off the Ladybug with your laser pen 59
Suggest you should keep looking for Frankie 61
Run outside 63
Decide to join him 64
Refuse the Bugman's offer 66
Press the arrow 70
Press the red button 73
Press the green button 77
Suggest you follow the trail of the class and the Bugman 80
Tell the journalists you think the Bugman has a hideout under the elephant statue 83
Tell the journalists you're just a kid on a school trip 86

Follow Frankie through the staff only door	87
Try to grab the remote	88
Put your hands up	93
Race over to add sugar to the water bowl	96
Help Frankie use the string as reins	98
Keep pulling on the butterfly reins	99
Tell Frankie to stop pulling on the butterfly reins	102
Chase after Ms Xavier to get the remote back	105
Press the black button and jump in front of the transmogrifier	107
Press the gray button and jump in front of the transmogrifier	111
Stay on the butterfly's back to distract the Bugman	116
Attack the ant with the mini screwdriver	122
Continue through to the rest of the exhibit	124
Team up with Spider Girl	126
Grab the remote	129
Rush to save Ms Xavier	134
Help Rose distract the Bugman	136
Team up with the boy drawing the weta	141
Ask Jeremy Wilder, "Why?"	143
Join WOS as a spy	148
Become an entomologist	151
Stay silent and see what happens	153
Help Eric look for Ms Xavier	155
Tell the Bugman where Eric went	158
Keep quiet and hope Eric and Ms Xavier are okay	162
Obey instructions and grab a terrarium	166
You choose: Ant. Grasshopper	169
You choose: Bee. Caterpillar	173
You choose: Cat. Lepidoptera	174
Insect Glossary	176
Sign Up for New Adventures	181
Books by A.J. Ponder	182

First edition 2018

Cover Art: Imojen Faith Hancock
ISBN: 978-1700157942

29 Laura Ave, Brooklyn, Wellington 6021,
New Zealand
phantomfeatherpress@gmail.com

Made in the USA
Middletown, DE
21 May 2020